The Pirate Raiders

C.G. Mosley

SEVERED PRESS
HOBART TASMANIA

The Pirate Raiders

ISBN: 978-1-925597-95-0

Chapter 1

It seemed that July 6, 1717, would surely be my last day on God's earth. Four days prior, my ship, a modest sloop named *Rebecca*, was overtaken by a man-of-war from the Royal Navy. My entire crew and I were taken prisoner. That's not to say that every member of my crew was still alive when we were taken—quite the contrary. Out of seventy-one men, only thirty of us lived to face the harsh consequences of piracy.

As soon as the man-of-war dropped anchor at Port Royal, Jamaica, I was separated from the survivors of my crew and placed in a cell that made it impossible for me to know of their well-being. This was not a surprise to me, for I was their captain and pirate captains were commonly separated from their crew immediately after capture. All I could do was sit and wonder, but deep in my gut a little voice told me that what remained of my loyal crew were now probably just as dead as the others.

I found myself shackled and struggling to walk down the long stone hallway that undoubtedly led to my trial that would in turn lead to my execution. The notion of having a trial for a pirate seemed like a waste of time. Very seldom did any pirate manage to escape the gallows. I'd accepted my fate as soon as I was taken prisoner. That didn't mean I was happy about it. I was literally sick to my stomach, but there was nothing I could do about it.

I thought about the skeletons I'd seen on occasion hanging in iron cages that greeted anyone who visited Port Royal. The skeletons were former pirates, and their rotting corpses were hung near the entrance of the harbor as a clear warning. Pirates were not welcome in Port Royal and if any were caught, they would be hanged.

Imagining myself hanging in one of those iron cages did nothing to settle my nausea.

There were four guards escorting me, two in front and two behind. We finally reached a pair of large wooden doors and the guards in front shoved them open with ease. The guards behind guided me to a single wooden chair placed in front of a large table.

On the other side of the table sat the governor of Port Royal and several other old men who I could only assume were his assistants.

"Mr. William Reeves, I presume," the governor said in a most boring tone.

"I am indeed William Reeves," I answered.

The governor had dark, beady eyes that gazed upon me over a long, pointy nose. I estimated he was approximately sixty years old. He seemed to look down on me over that long nose.

"Have a seat, young man," the governor said, motioning to the chair behind me.

I sat down and took a moment to rub the soreness around my wrists and ankles.

"I am Governor Charles Winters, and I will be presiding over the trial set forth on this sixth day of July in the year 1717. It seems that a vessel of the Royal Navy spotted a pirate ship while in route to Port Royal. They engaged in a brief battle with said pirate ship. The battle resulted in vast casualties and ultimately the pirate ship, the…" The governor turned his attention to a document laid out on the table before him. "Ah, here it is… the sloop named *Rebecca* was not salvageable and soon sank into the ocean depths. Thirty men were taken prisoner; you were among them, Mr. Reeves."

There was a long silence and the governor continued to peer at me with those beady eyes as if he were awaiting some sort of response from me. I wasn't sure what he wanted to hear. I was a dead man and I knew it. Knowing this made me defiant and I decided right then that I would volunteer no information to the governor or anyone else for that matter. If he wanted to sit in silence and wait for me to speak, then he would be waiting for a long while. A few more moments passed and the governor let out a deep sigh.

"It seems you have nothing to say," he said. "I know who you are, Captain Reeves. Or should I call you Captain Redd?"

I swallowed when he pronounced my name, and the room was so deadly quiet that my gulp seemed to echo loudly. I remained silent and although I must have seemed distraught, I did the best I could to keep my composure.

"We've questioned your men, but to be honest, they refused to reveal your identity. They were tortured and beaten, but those men are fiercely loyal to their captain."

The governor seemed to get a sick pleasure as he went on to describe the ways he tortured my crew. I tuned most of it out. I didn't want to know what sort of horrors they went through. I was grateful to them for wanting to protect me, but I felt incredible guilt too.

"Your men never once hinted that their leader was the notorious Captain Redd," the governor continued. "Unfortunately, the Royal Navy crew that overtook your ship was unable to plunder its contents before it sank to the bottom of the ocean. Mr. Reeves, there was seemingly nothing available to us to confirm you are indeed Captain Redd."

I couldn't help but smile. No one knew the real name of Captain Redd. I liked it that way and I wasn't going to volunteer that information now. The secret would go with me to my grave.

The governor continued, "I've always heard that Captain Redd got his name from the fiery red hair that adorns the top of his head," he said, eyeing the fiery red hair atop my head. "Unfortunately, that's not enough evidence to confirm my suspicions. So little is known about Captain Redd; the color of his hair could be like any other number of stories that are floating around about him. Are you familiar with any of these stories, Mr. Reeves?"

I remained silent and just stared at him. It didn't seem to bother him.

"One story I've heard is that once Captain Redd and his crew were surrounded by three Spanish warships. Somehow Redd and his crew overtook each ship, one at a time, until the sea around them turned red with Spanish blood and afterward the pirates made off with a Spanish galleon loaded with untold piles of gold. I've heard that gold is still hidden somewhere on a tiny island in the vast ocean."

The story the governor had heard was for the most part true. Except it was four Spanish warships, and we spent the vast majority of that gold. However, there were a couple of chests buried on a small island near Tortuga. Nevertheless, I remained stone-faced and said nothing.

"There was one other story I heard that gave a clue concerning the identity of Captain Redd," the governor said. "A merchant ship sailed into port several months back and the captain told me a story of a pirate ship that robbed him of all of his medical supplies. He said the pirate ship flew a black flag adorned with a human skeleton. The skeleton had a cutlass in hand and a red skull. Mr. Reeves, you can imagine how my eyes widened as I realized that the merchant ship captain had just described the Jolly Roger most commonly associated with Captain Redd."

I swallowed again but remained calm.

"As I said before, Mr. Reeves, the Royal Navy was unable to search the sloop before it sank. However, they did manage to salvage one vital piece of evidence."

My eyebrow arched as the governor leaned over and picked something up off the floor. As soon as he arose, I knew exactly what it was and I knew the secrecy of Captain Redd's identity was gone.

"I believe this belongs to you, does it not?"

The governor grabbed the corners of the cloth and shook it until the folded black flag opened completely. It was Captain Redd's flag... my flag. The Jolly Roger was the one way to identify all pirates and I was no different. It was just as that merchant ship captain had described it to the governor: a skeleton with a red skull holding a cutlass.

I took a deep breath and considered my next move. There was no need to continue my stance of remaining silent and denying everything. Clearly, the governor knew all along that I was the notorious Captain Redd. I looked at him, and I looked at the other old men that flanked him left and right. They hadn't said a word since I'd been in the room. Then something else occurred to me. Why wasn't my trial being held before a Vice Admiralty court? Colonial governors had not presided over trials such as mine for over fifteen years. Something was off about all of it and I wanted to get to the bottom of it immediately. I began to chuckle lightly.

"You got me governor," I said, clapping my hands together in applause. "I am the one and only Captain Redd."

The governor slapped the table in a joyous fashion. He was clearly happy to hear me say the words.

"I knew it," he said cheerfully.

"You were just too smart for me sir," I continued. "However, I must confess that I am somewhat confused by this court arrangement."

Governor Winters's joyful mood suddenly subsided and was immediately replaced with worry—the kind of worry one gets when they know they've been caught doing something dishonest. In fact, I imagined I had a similar expression across my own face moments earlier when the realization set in that I'd been found out.

"What are you referring to, Mr. Reeves?"

It annoyed me that the good governor defiantly refused to refer to me as Captain Reeves, especially after I had made it known that I wasn't just any ordinary pirate captain. So it didn't bother me at all to return the disrespect toward Governor Winters.

"Well, *Mr.* Winters," I said with a smirk. "I believe King George would be displeased to know that the colony you oversee does not conduct its trials under a Vice Admiralty court."

The governor's face began to turn red and the rage building within him was evident in his eyes. The other men at the table began to move uncomfortably in their chairs.

"And just what do you know about a Vice Admiralty court, pirate?" Governor Winters snarled.

His mood didn't rattle me the slightest bit.

"I know that for at least the past fifteen years every pirate trial has been overseen by dignitaries and sea captains from right here in Port Royal," I replied. "I know many sea captains and high ranking officials that reside in this town. I don't recognize a single one of the men seated at the table with you."

Governor Winters's looked toward the guards on either side of me. For an instant, I thought he was going to ask one of them to assault me. Instead, he asked them to leave the room. After a moment of bewilderment, all four guards exited the room, leaving only Governor Winters, his assistants, and me.

A normal person in my position would've surely felt fear at this moment. I, on the other hand, felt nothing of the sort. I'd already accepted that this day would be my last. If I was going to die by the hand of a corrupt colonial governor, so be it.

"Pirate, you are correct," the governor said, suddenly much calmer. "This court is nothing more than a clever trick."

As you can imagine, I was suddenly very confused.

"A trick?" I asked.

Governor Winters nodded and suddenly stood from the table.

"I had to make sure you were who I thought you were," he replied. "Now I'm sure."

I shook my head, still unable to process what was going on.

"Governor, I'm afraid I don't understand."

"Captain, it was of extreme importance that I made sure you were Captain Redd because the task I have for you is daunting to say the least."

"Daunting? Task?" I said, still confused.

The governor hastily strolled around the table and stopped in front of me. He reached in the pocket of his long, black robe and retrieved a small key. He inserted the key in my shackles, freeing me.

Awestruck, it took a moment for me to find my next words. However, there was one obvious question that I wanted answered immediately.

"Will I be executed?"

Governor Winters returned to his chair and stared at me with those beady eyes. After a long moment, he gave me a cryptic answer.

"That depends," he said flatly.

"On what?"

"I have a most dangerous task for you, Captain Redd. The reason I had to make sure you were who you are is because I truly believe you are the only man that can accomplish this task. The fate of your life is very simple: complete the task I give you and you will be granted a royal pardon."

"That sounds wonderful," I replied dryly. "However, I think you should know I'm a package deal. What about what remains of my crew?"

The governor huffed, and I got the feeling he wasn't ready to discuss the fate of my crew just yet. Nevertheless, I didn't back down. "To complete a dangerous task, I need my men at my side," I stated forcefully. "Unfortunately, you've already complicated matters and made this task you speak of even more dangerous than it already is."

Governor Winters continued to stare at me, confusion etched on his face.

"Your men have already killed a significant portion of my crew," I said in an effort to erase his confusion. "It is imperative that what remains of my crew are also released and allowed to accompany me on your 'task.' Furthermore, they are to be granted pardons too."

Governor Winters suddenly slammed his fist down on the table and bared clenched teeth.

"How dare you give me orders, pirate? You are not in a position to bargain with me!"

"And you, sir, must need my help pretty badly to put yourself in the position you now find yourself in," I replied calmly. "You are requesting my help. I am telling you what I need to help you."

"There are plenty of worthy seamen I will make available to you that are superior to that band of misfits you call a crew," he snarled in reply.

"It doesn't work that way, Governor. I need my crew or there is no deal."

As soon as I said the words, I couldn't believe I'd said them. The governor was offering me a golden opportunity to escape an execution I truly believed was a certainty mere minutes ago. What was I thinking spewing orders at him and giving him an ultimatum? He eyed me sharply, no doubt reading my thoughts.

"Very well," he said finally, sighing. "You will have what remains of your wretched crew... all twenty-eight of them. It amazes me that you're barking orders at *me* when you have no idea what I have in store for you."

"Forgive me, Governor, but I woke up this morning under the false assumption that it would be my last. My main focus these last few moments have been on nothing but how to survive the day. Fortunately, I just checked that off my to-do list. Now on to the next chore: how can I, and what is left of my illustrious band of pirates, help you?"

"Spare me the theatrical nonsense, Captain Redd. You are not completely free until you complete my task, and do not think you'll be able to sail into the sunset without doing what I ask. The task will require you to retrieve a certain object and return it to me. I'll give you six months to achieve this. If I do not hear back from you in six months' time, I will put a bounty on your head large enough that every pirate and privateer from Tortuga to Madagascar will be looking for you."

I nodded in agreement. "I'm a man of my word, Governor."

He breathed what seemed to be a sigh of relief and slumped into his chair. He believed me, and it seemed that my words lifted a great weight from his shoulders. Governor Winters suddenly seemed older and more tired. Something big was troubling him.

"Captain Redd, do you ever read the Bible?"

I blinked twice as I allowed the question to sink in. "Of course, I have read passages from the Bible. However, I will not mislead you. It has been quite a while since I've studied any of the King James."

The governor nodded at me, and his scowl returned. "I figured as much. Given your current profession, I'm surprised you've read any of it at all. Nevertheless, are you familiar with the story of King Solomon?"

"I am not, but if he was a king, then there must have been treasure of some kind or another involved. You have my undivided attention."

"Ah yes, King Solomon collected piles and piles of treasure, but none of the gold is my concern at this moment."

"Well it concerns *me*," I replied. "Where is this King Solomon's gold located?"

"No one knows, and I will remind you yet again that the gold is not my concern, nor should it be yours. What is of grave importance is a particular ring that once adorned Solomon's hand."

"A golden ring?" I asked, pretending to be excited.

"A magical ring," he replied dryly. "A signet ring that, according to legend, gave King Solomon the power to control demons, and it even gave him the ability to speak to animals. King Solomon's ring has fallen into evil hands, and I employ you to get it back and return it to me on behalf of King George."

For a brief moment, I must admit that I truly believed the old governor was having a little fun with me. However, when his serious expression never ceased, it became quite apparent that my assumption was incorrect. There was a long silence. I wasn't sure how to respond to his claims. I knew of magic—a certain sort, anyway. Voo doo magic was well known throughout the Caribbean, but I'd never given it much thought. I didn't know for sure if it was real, nor did I deny its existence; I fell somewhere in the middle.

"How exactly did this magic ring you speak of fall into evil hands?" I asked.

Governor Winters let out another tired sigh before he spoke. "It's nearly impossible to separate fact from fiction… there are so many different stories regarding the ring. Here is the legend as I know it: King Solomon's ring was unearthed near Jerusalem over 500 years ago, during the Crusades. It is believed that the ring was used by the Crusaders to unleash a multitude of demons upon the Muslim forces. Although the Crusaders were fighting in the name of Christ, they felt that their use of the ring was justifiable since their foe was unholy and unworthy to remain in the Holy Land.

"For a time, the ring's power allowed the Crusaders to gain the upper hand over their Muslim enemies and they enjoyed several victories. Unfortunately, the victories were only short term, and it seemed that they were won with a heavy price. It is believed that God punished the Crusaders for turning to the ring and its demonic powers in their effort to claim the Holy Land in His name. It is widely believed that use of the ring is the reason the Crusades were lost."

"What happened to the ring after that?" I asked anxiously.

"The ring was locked in a silver chest and moved from castle to castle over the past 500 years. Legend says that the chest was guarded at all times by four of the king's best soldiers. No one dared open the chest for fear of what the consequences could be for England and whoever the reigning queen or king was at the time."

"Over time, the legend of King Solomon's ring began to ring less true, until finally most people dismissed the story altogether as nothing more than a child's bedtime story. About seventy-five years ago, the practice of guarding the ring ceased.

"Before I go any further, there is something you must understand. King George is a very superstitious soul. When he took the throne, he made it clear early on that he did not like the idea of having the ring in the same quarters as him. He requested to speak to the captain of the next ship headed for Port Royal. In a private meeting, that captain was ordered to dispose of the ring into the depths of the Atlantic Ocean near the midway point of the voyage."

"Apparently, things didn't go according to plan," I said.

The governor crossed his arms and shook his head regretfully. "No, it seems the captain of that ship had other plans. He sold the ring at sea to a pirate. The Royal Navy captain and his dreadful crew collected a lion's share of gold for the ring, but they made a very serious mistake."

I cocked my head sideways, puzzled about what the governor was referring to.

"They should've never trusted a bloody pirate," he said sharply.

I nodded. "Let me guess: the corrupt captain and his crew of fools didn't get very far with that gold, did they?"

"No sooner had the wind began to fill their sails, the pirate captain put the ring to good use and called upon a tentacled monstrosity from the depths of the Atlantic Ocean."

"The kraken," I whispered.

"The poor ship and the crew never stood a chance. It was all destroyed in mere minutes."

I shook my head and chewed my lip as I digested the governor's words. There was no good reason for him to make up a story like the one I'd just heard. I believed him; the somber expression on his face could not be faked. The governor was truly concerned about what the coming days held for him and the rest of the world. It seemed he was relying on me of all people to make things right. For a brief instance, the gallows didn't seem so bad anymore. There was only one part of the governor's story that didn't make sense.

"If this pirate captain you speak of had a beast of the sea destroy a Royal Navy ship in the middle of the Atlantic, how do you possibly know so many details of the incident?"

"I know because there was one survivor," the governor replied. "He was found floating on part of the wreckage by a passing merchant ship and brought to Port Royal. He told us everything."

I took a step toward the governor, suddenly intrigued by the news of this survivor. "May I speak with him?"

The governor looked toward the floor and slowly shook his head. "I'm afraid that will not be possible," he said. "The young man was injured gravely by a splinter from the mizzen mast. He died the day after our interrogation."

I frowned at the news. "That's unfortunate," I said. "I suppose there is only one other question that needs asking."

"Yes," the governor replied. "You want to know the identity of the pirate captain that currently holds possession of the most powerful ring in the entire world."

I waited anxiously for him to tell me. I prayed that it wasn't Blackbeard, and yet I knew there was another pirate captain sailing the seas that was worse than he. *Surely not*, I thought hopefully.

"The witness was very certain that the pirate captain was none other than Winston Trimble," the governor said solemnly.

Damn! My nausea returned; I felt incredibly sick. The governor must have noticed the change of color in my face because he quickly urged me to sit down. I followed his advice, and although sitting down did help, the nausea didn't leave me. *Why oh why did it have to be Captain Trimble?*

"Now perhaps you see why I went to extreme measures to bring you here and why I had no choice but to ask for your help with this unfortunate matter," Governor Winters said in a tone that suggested we were suddenly friends instead of foes.

"Governor, I beg your pardon, but you haven't *asked* me to do anything," I snapped back. "I seem to have very little choice in the matter."

He stared back at me steely eyed and began to revert to the bitter old man I'd met when I first entered the room. "Pirate, there is always a choice," he answered coldly. "If you refuse, you and your crew will die. If you choose to embark on this task, you will have the opportunity to live out your days and leave this world when God chooses the time of your death, not me."

I wanted to curse him at that moment but thought better of it. "I see your point." That was all I could muster. "Captain Trimble flies under a red flag. There are no pirates in the Caribbean that are his ally. Surely you can understand my concern, Governor. You *do* know the meaning of the red flag?"

"Of course I know the meaning of it," he barked in response. "The red jack means there will be no mercy… no quarter given! It means death to all that encounter Captain Trimble's ship. I understand the monumental task before you, Captain Redd. However, you have quite a reputation yourself and have proven to be very resourceful in dire situations. I will give you a worthy ship and anything else you require."

I stood there with my mouth gaped open like a fool. I didn't know what to say. I didn't know if I was currently feeling fear or anger. I imagined giving this news to my crew mere minutes after they rejoiced of the news of their freedom. I could already hear Langley's barrage of insults and curse words that would no doubt spew from his cracked and chapped lips. None of them would want any part of chasing after Trimble and his ship *Sea Witch*. It would be my burden as captain to convince them otherwise.

"Give me a quill and parchment. I will make a list of the items I require," I said at last.

The governor smiled a wide, toothy grin. "I'm glad to hear that," he said. "Be sure to thank God tonight for sparing your life when you look up at the stars. And if you ask nicely, He may just assist you in killing Trimble."

The governor began to laugh and I knew he was right. The only way I'd get that ring away from Captain Trimble would be to kill him. I truly believed only God could make that happen.

Chapter 2

The matter of my crew was resolved swiftly. As soon as the governor and I had concluded our meeting, I was escorted back to the prison and given the honor of releasing my men. They were, understandably, relieved to see me again. My loyal helmsman, Oliver Langley, was the first to greet me. Langley was forty years old, his skin the color of copper, a direct result of a lifetime at sea. I firmly believed there was no helmsman anywhere in the Caribbean that was as gifted as he; however, he had one flaw. He drank more rum than any man I'd ever met. There were many times when this affected his abilities at the helm of my ship. Still, he was a loyal and trusted friend. He would be at the wheel as long as he desired to be, and I would do what I could to manage his unquenchable thirst for rum.

"Cap'n Redd, we feared you'd already fallen victim to the gallows," he said, relieved to see me alive and well. It was probably the soberest I'd seen him in ten years.

"Langley, you all know me better than that," I replied, clasping a hand on his bony shoulder. "Have you and the others been treated fairly?"

Langley's weathered face dropped to the ground so low that all I could see was the gray hair atop his head. When his head arose back up, he gazed into my eyes and there was a fury behind them that I hadn't seen before. "These scurvy dogs drubbed us repeatedly and threatened to hang us if we didn't tell them who you really were."

I glanced over at the two soldiers who had escorted me to the prison cells. "They beat you, did they?" I said with a snarl. The guards said nothing, but one returned a smug look my way that suggested he held no regrets. I leaned over to Langley and spoke just loud enough where he could hear me. "We'll deal with the vermin later." He nodded and his anger seemed to subside. "Where is Gordon?" I asked, scanning the rugged group of pirates in front of me.

"Alive and well, no thanks to you," an eloquent voice called out from the back of the group.

Gordon Littleton was only a few years my senior, but he seemed far older. He did not fit in at all with the rest of the pirates that stood before me and there was a good reason for that. At one time, Gordon was employed as a navigator for the East India Trading Company. As fate would have it, our paths crossed five years ago when my crew and I intercepted the galleon on which Gordon was aboard. It was the luxury goods we were after, but the crew was unwilling to give up the treasure without a fight. So fight we did, and although we won the battle, it came with a price. Ned Plinkton, my long-time navigator, was mortally wounded. We happily shoved off with our treasure that day, and since we suddenly found ourselves without a navigator, we took Gordon Littleton too.

I fully expected the first few days and weeks to be a very trying time. I didn't know if Gordon had a family, nor did I know how willing he would be to cooperate with what we asked of him. It was somewhat of a pleasant surprise when Gordon signed the articles so willingly, and he did everything that was asked of him. For a year, he kept to himself, said very little, and I didn't bother to speak to him much either. I saw him as something of a skulk, content with wallowing in his own self-pity. He never even took a sip of rum during the entire year.

We finally had a lengthy conversation during his second year in which he admitted to me a startling revelation. Gordon had no family back home, at least not anymore, because he'd murdered his wife the month before I'd taken him captive. He'd found her with another man the night before he was to leave home. He killed the both of them, the wife and her lover, and did nothing to hide his crime before he left his home for the final time. He admitted that he'd been terrified about returning home after his time at sea. Gordon was certain the gallows would be awaiting him upon his return.

The morning he saw the sails of my pirate ship on the horizon, he accepted that whatever happened would be his punishment from God for his crime. It was not a surprise to him when we forced him to join the crew, and although the life he now lived was disgusting to him, he accepted it as a consequence for what he had done. As the years went by, Gordon became more and more comfortable with his place on my ship and eventually warmed up to the rest of the crew. He even began to partake in the rum rationing.

There was, and I assumed always would be, a cockiness about him that occasionally got under my skin. Perhaps it was the way he spoke and the time he took to make certain each strand of blond hair upon his head was lying perfectly. Nevertheless, he was a valuable member of my crew, and he and Langley became my most trusted advisors. It was no surprise to me that he was now standing in the shadows, behind the rest of the crew.

"Gordon, come forward so I can see your swabby face," I commanded cheerfully. Gordon stepped through the crowd and for the first time I'd known him, his golden hair was in complete disarray, his face bloodied and bruised. "I see that you were mistreated also," I said grimly.

"Aye, captain, all of us were."

"Gordon was drubbed worst of all," Langley chimed in. "They mistook his well-kempt hair to mean he would be the softest and easiest of us to break."

"They were wrong," Gordon said firmly. "I told them nothing, captain."

I scanned over the rest of my tired and beaten crew. I was moved by the lengths they had gone to protect me even though they were unaware whether I was alive or dead. I reached forward and gave Gordon a bear hug.

"I vow to all of you that I will not forget what you've endured for me. I am indebted to each of you. I hope your freedom is a consolation for what you've gone through. There will be plenty of rum to go around tonight!"

The mention of rum made Langley smile. "Point me to it," he said anxiously.

"There will be time for that later," I answered with a smile. "I need to speak with you and Gordon in private." I turned to the others. "As for the rest of you, I've made arrangements for your personal belongings to be returned to you at the front gate when you exit this wretched place. That includes your weapons and any coin each of you had on your person when we were taken captive.

I urge you all to go out and get yourselves a hot meal. Go out, find a lady of the evening, and drink until your heart is content. Tomorrow morning, we set sail!"

The men cheered and then a hulking, mammoth of a man stepped forward. "How did you manage this, Cap'n?" he asked in his deep, growling voice. The man was Hale Woodrow, the ship carpenter. He was a good, strong man, but dimwitted and almost childlike.

I moved beside him and patted him on the back. I had to stand on my toes to do so. "Go out and enjoy yourself tonight, Mr. Woodrow. Everything will be explained tomorrow," I assured him. "That goes for all of you. Let's meet at the docks an hour after sunrise."

The men filed out, picking up their cutlasses, pistols, and other belongings as they left the building. I couldn't help but wonder if any of them would show up in the morning on time. It would have been wise of me to forbid them from drinking on this night, but how could I? They'd been tortured for me. Besides, I knew something they did not. There were no plans to shove off from Port Royal until the afternoon. The morning would be spent stocking the ship I was promised. Surely by the time we really were ready to set sail, all the men would be accounted for.

I was the last to retrieve my weapons and hat. I slapped the leather tricorn on my pants leg and a plume of dust wisped into the air. I didn't feel complete without that hat, and I smiled as I put it on. Now I felt whole again.

Just as I stepped into the night with Langely and Gordon at my side and allowed myself a moment to enjoy a cool ocean breeze off the bay, I heard my name called out from somewhere behind me. I turned to see one of the guards approaching, and for a second I feared the governor had had a change of heart. I was unable to see the man's face until he was three feet away and the light from a nearby oil lamp illuminated his rugged features. His eyebrows were dark and bushy and he had a mustache to match. There was no expression upon his face and I found myself reaching for my cutlass.

"Captain Redd Reeves, Governor Winters requested that I deliver a message to you at once," he said in a gravelly voice. He reached into his red coat and retrieved an envelope. I took it gently and examined the wax seal. It was the governor's.

What the devil is this? I just left the man...

"Have a good evening, Captain," the guard said as he spun on his heel and strolled back into the bowels of the stone building.

"Well go ahead, let's have a look," Langley urged.

I ripped the envelope open and removed the parchment inside. I scanned over the governor's urgent message as quickly as I could, admiring the beautiful penmanship as I read.

"Well, what does it say?" Gordon asked.

I ignored him, immediately crumpled the parchment up in my fist, and made use of the nearby oil lamp mounted on the nearby sconce. Gordon and Langley looked on curiously as the document quickly disintegrated into ash.

"Why in the blue hell did you burn it?" Gordon asked, bewildered.

"I can't explain yet, not here," I replied in a whisper, even though no one else was around. "Besides, I have much more to tell you before we discuss what was on that parchment. Let's find a more suitable place to talk, shall we?"

I escorted Oliver Langley (who was not very happy about missing out on the night's festivities) and Gordon Littleton to a tavern near the edge of town that overlooked the bay. The three of us entered the dining hall and settled around a small, candle-lit table in the corner of the scarcely populated room. The tavern, the Parrot's Landing, was a well-known pirate hideout, but it would provide me the amount of seclusion I desired to brief Langley and Gordon on why we were being released and what was expected of us.

Pirates are a superstitious bunch, but I conveniently left out the supernatural details of the ring we were after for two distinct reasons: First, I saw no reason to burden the men with a tale of the ring calling up the kraken and other demonic beings when I myself wasn't completely sure the stories were true. And secondly, the notion of hunting down Captain Winston Trimble would probably scare them enough by itself. I underestimated the effect of the second reason.

"You're a fool, William," Gordon spat at me when he heard the news. The sheer fact that he called me William was a clear indication of how furious he was. "You should've just left us to die in that prison. I would rather die with a noose around my neck than with my entrails splattered across the deck of the *Sea Witch*."

Langley chugged rum from the wooden mug he held tightly in his bony fingers as Gordon spoke. When he finished, he slammed the mug down on the table and used his sleeve to wipe the moisture from his lips and chin. "Cap'n, I have to agree with Gordon. If we go after Trimble, we've doomed ourselves to Davy Jones's locker."

I leaned back in my chair and crossed my arms. After hearing the both of them voice their concerns, I was thankful that I trusted my gut and left out the supernatural parts. "If we refuse this task, we have still doomed ourselves to Davy Jones's locker. At least this way we have a chance," I pleaded. "Winston Trimble, a rogue maggot he may be, but does he or does he not bleed the same as you and me?"

"Aye, he does," Langley replied.

"Then if he bleeds, he can be killed."

Gordon shook his head and cursed under his breath. "Captain Trimble flies a red jack upon his mainmast, William. Do you have an inkling of what that means?"

I opened my mouth to speak, but Gordon continued before I could.

"I bet a brig doesn't even exist below the decks of the *Sea Witch*. Trimble has no use for one." Gordon stared at me and sighed. "If we are unable to gain the upper hand quickly, he will slay each and every one of us. It will probably be a slow and painful death. I've heard that Captain Trimble cuts off flesh from his captives and makes them eat it in front of him."

I leaned forward, resting both arms on the table. "Then we better make damn sure we gain the upper hand," I said calmly. "I like my flesh exactly where it is."

Gordon thought a moment and stroked his smooth chin. "I want you to take a moment and consider something."

I nodded for him to continue. "I'm listening."

"Governor Winters has the entire Royal Navy at his fingertips. Isn't that right?"

"It is," I replied.

"Then why on earth is he calling upon a pirate to seize another pirate?"

Gordon stared at me and waited for a response. I wanted to tell him that Governor Winters claimed he had already lost one Royal Navy ship to the power of the ring Captain Trimble possessed, but of course I'd left the supernatural details out. "He called upon us for two reasons," I finally answered. "Firstly, a pirate that is fighting for a chance to live, as we all are, is far more dangerous than any buffoon sworn to the Royal Navy."

"And the second reason?" Gordon inquired.

"Because I'm the infamous Captain Redd Reeves, of course," I said, swelling with pride.

"That you are," Langley agreed.

Gordon was unable to stifle a smile. It was at that moment, I knew I had the both of them on my side. "Gentlemen, I've never steered you wrong before, have I?"

They both looked at each other. Gordon reluctantly shook his head and tapped his fingers on the table. "No, Captain, you have not."

"I'm not going to start tonight either," I assured them.

A barmaid refilled Langley's mug, but instead of chugging it down, he stared into the dark liquid as he thought. Gordon continued to drum his fingers on the table and allowed his eyes to move toward the window overlooking the Atlantic Ocean. They were both still mulling it over.

"The rest of the men will be a lot more comfortable with this if they know the two of you are confident about it," I continued. "For there to be any chance of success, I need the two of you on board that ship with me. So, what's it going to be? Can I count on the two of you?"

Langley snatched up the wooden mug, sloshing the liquid all over the table. He drank what was left in a matter of seconds before slamming the mug back on to the wooden surface again. "Of course, I'm with you, Cap'n."

I smiled, and he smiled a snaggle-toothed grin back in reply. "What about you, Gordon?"

Gordon put his elbows on the table and rested his face in his palms. He drew a deep breath before moving his hands away again. "Of course I'm in," he said quietly.

"Very well then; I knew I could count on the both of you," I said proudly. "Now that that is out of the way, there is another reason why I wanted the two of you to accompany me and not partake in the night's festivities."

Gordon and Langley stared at me with worried expressions. They clearly weren't interested in any more surprises tonight. Unfortunately, I had one more. It was time to discuss the message I'd received, and then burned, from the governor.

"I think that now is the appropriate time to discuss the message I burned outside of Fort Charles," I said. Langley and Gordon leaned forward on the table with obvious intrigue as they waited anxiously for me to continue. "There's no doubt that Governor Winters wants us to succeed in finding Captain Trimble as soon as possible," I continued. "The message that was delivered to me indicated that a member of Trimble's crew was recently picked up on a tiny spot of land near the Leeward Islands."

"He was marooned?" Gordon asked.

"Apparently so," I replied. "The pirate goes by the name Andy Bonnet. According to the governor's message, he was captured several weeks ago and brought to Port Royal. He was imprisoned at Fort Charles and tried for his crimes of piracy earlier this morning. It seems that Mr. Bonnet was found guilty and will be taken to Gallows Point early tomorrow morning to be hanged."

"That's interesting," Gordon said. "But I fail to see how this news is supposed to help us."

"I think it's safe to assume that Mr. Bonnet may have information that could, at the very least, point us in the general direction of Captain Trimble. He would know valuable information regarding Trimble's habits."

"Habits?" Langley asked, the rum beginning to slur his voice.

"Yes," I replied. "His favorite taverns, brothels, and even his favorite spots to careen his ship. I'm sure Bonnet has some idea of where Trimble was headed before he was marooned. Any information he could provide may give us a heading that we may have otherwise spent days or weeks trying to find on our own."

"Are you saying that the governor will allow us to question Andy Bonnet before he is hanged?" Gordon asked.

"No."

Gordon gave me a blank stare. "Then how on God's earth is this information supposed to help us?"

"The message stated that Andy Bonnet will be transported by prison carriage tonight around the nine o'clock hour. Two guards will be moving him from Fort Charles to a small prison near Gallows' Point."

Gordon began to shake his head as he finally understood where this was going. "Captain, you can't possibly be serious. You want Langley and me to assist you in helping this man escape?"

"Aye, you're finally catching on," I replied with a smile. "The governor even provided the route that they're planning to take, and I've got it all right here," I said, pointing to the side of my head. "The final line of the message instructed me to destroy it. It's obvious that Governor Winters wants us to go after Bonnet, but he doesn't want any part in it. If we're caught, we'll probably hang right next to Bonnet in the morning."

"Then we better not get caught," Langley said, standing up from the table. "What are we waiting for? Let's go."

God love Oliver Langley, I thought. *Get a little rum in him and he becomes invincible.*

"That's the spirit," Gordon said, his words oozing sarcasm. "Follow him like the dumb sheep that you are."

Langley narrowed his eyes on Gordon and clenched his fists. If I didn't talk fast, the two of them would be scrapping like wolves and my plans for the night would be damned. "Langley, what Gordon is trying to say," I said softly, "is that we need to discuss our plan before going at this blindly. However, I do appreciate your bravery," I added for good measure.

The crow's feet next to Langley's eyes softened along with the rest of his expression. "Yes," he said, sitting back down. "I suppose that is a good idea."

Gordon rolled his eyes. His sour expression indicated he wanted no part of this and probably wanted to be anywhere but here right now. Nevertheless, I told them my plan.

"According to the message, the prison carriage always takes the same route to Gallows' Point. They will travel east along Parade Tower Street until they reach the Old Church. They will then turn right on High Street and make their way through the Produce District. The very next left will lead them just beyond Gallows' Point and to nearby Marshall Sea Prison. That is their final destination."

"That particular prison is between Fort Carlisle and Fort Rupert," Gordon stated, a genuinely concerned look on his face. "Marshall Sea Prison is only half a mile from either fort. I certainly hope you plan on breaking Mr. Bonnet out before you get on the other side of the Market District."

"I intend to do just that," I replied with a smile. "I'm pleased to learn you're familiar with that end of town, Gordon." Pirates tended to stay away from the eastern end of town. If the courthouse, prisons, and forts weren't enough to keep them away, the rotting corpses hanging at Gallows' Point were.

"As you know," Gordon replied, "I was not always a pirate. I spent my fair share of time on that end of the city back when I was still an honest seaman."

"Your knowledge of that part of the city will serve you well tonight. Now," I continued, "as you pointed out, I will need to free Mr. Bonnet before the prison carriage makes it through the Market District. There is a very large oak tree near the Old Church graveyard. The branches reach out over the street like an old man's withered fingers. When carriages pass under the tree, I swear that they don't clear the branches by any more than four or five feet. Gentlemen, when the prison carriage passes under that tree tonight, I will be waiting on one of those branches. I'll drop right onto the roof of the carriage and the guards will not even know I'm there."

Langley smiled a wide, yellow-toothed grin. "That's mighty clever, Cap'n," he said.

"You may as well be chum getting thrown to sharks," Gordon quipped, his words erasing Langley's smile. "May I ask just how do you plan on overtaking the two guards? They will no doubt be armed with swords and pistols, or maybe even a musket!"

"Right you are, Gordon. The only way I'll be able to overtake those buggers is if something, or someone, distracts them first," I said, staring at him. "That's where *you* come in, my friend."

Gordon immediately held up his hands to wave me off. "No, no, Captain," he said nervously. "You don't need me to distract them." He looked at Langley and hooked a thumb toward him. "Sounds like a job for this boozy bloke."

I saw the anger begin to build in Langley again and I responded quickly to diffuse it. "I'm afraid that Langley has the most important job of all," I said.

Langley gave Gordon a narrow glance and leaned forward with a mixture of pride and unbridled anticipation etched on his weathered face. "Tell me, Cap'n... what do you need me to do?"

Chapter 3

Gordon retched as I smeared horse manure over his clothes, and worse yet, his face. I knew it had to be agonizing for a man so well kempt to endure what I was putting him through, but it was necessary for my plan to work.

"Please be still," I scolded him. "We've got to get you smelling bad enough that the guards don't want to get anywhere near you." I took a moment to glance around in both directions to make sure no one was watching us. We were crouched behind a massive tombstone in the center of the graveyard. Each row of tombstones, all of them different heights, reminded me of Langley's jagged teeth. As I thought of him, I hoped he would be in position and ready the very moment I needed him; our lives could depend on it.

Once we'd left the Parrot's Landing and out of Langley's earshot, Gordon wasted no time chastising me for giving him such an important job after he'd chugged down so much rum. I immediately reminded him that Langley seemed to be his best at the helm after he'd gotten a little rum in his belly. I knew my rebuttal did little to ease Gordon's concerns, but fortunately he dropped the subject altogether.

The large graveyard was a convenient place for us to prepare and wait for the right moment to take our positions before the prison carriage rolled down High Street. It was deserted and more importantly, it was near the Old Church.

"That should do it," I said, wiping what was left of the manure on my hand off on Gordon's pant leg.

"I'm beginning to think I got the short end of this stick," he said, frowning. "Remind me again why I agreed to do this."

"Fear of the noose," I replied thoughtfully. I snatched an old blue neckerchief from my coat pocket and folded it into a triangle. I quickly tied it around the back of my head and carefully positioned it to conceal my nose and mouth. "How do I look?"

"If you wanted to conceal your face, a coating of horse manure would've probably worked just as well," Gordon quipped.

I grinned, knowing full well he would be unable to see my expression beneath the neckerchief. "Let's get into position," I said, walking toward the large oak tree. Gordon grumbled incoherently and made his way to his hiding spot behind a large boulder resting under a thatch palm.

Fortunately, there was a limb low enough to the ground that allowed me to jump up and grab it with both hands. After pulling up the rest of my body, I carefully made my way to the other side of the tree and onto the large limb hanging over High Street. I stood on the branch and looked behind me. *No carriage yet.*

All I could do now was wait. I glanced down at the boulder Gordon was supposed to be hiding behind. The fact I was unable to see him gave me a brief sensation of panic, but then I remembered his total concealment was exactly what we were aiming for. I checked my chest once more to make certain that I had two pistols strapped there and ready to fire. If things went as planned, there would be no reason to fire either of the weapons, but I wouldn't hesitate to do so if it became necessary. Lastly, I took a moment to adjust the tricorn atop my head. I wanted to make sure it was as snug as possible; this little mission wouldn't be considered a success in my mind if I lost it.

While waiting, my thoughts drifted to Captain Winston Trimble. Finding the elusive captain would be difficult and very dangerous. I'd never met the man, but I, like many others, had heard countless stories about him. Legend had it that Captain Trimble didn't feel pain—emotional or physical. I'd never encountered any man that my pistol wouldn't slow down; it made my blood run cold to think of it. I hoped the stories I'd heard about him being unable to feel pain were nothing more than legend.

Sailors tremble at the sight of Captain Trimble. That was the catchy phrase worked in during almost any conversation regarding the ruthless captain. I'd heard stories about sailors committing suicide as soon as they spotted the red flag flying proudly above the *Sea Witch* on the horizon. I can't say that I blame them. Better to leave this world on your own terms than in the sick and demented ways Captain Trimble would have you go.

I felt a sudden jab of pain on my left hand, the result of a pebble Gordon had thrown to get my attention. I looked down at him and saw that he was motioning for me to look back. Before I even had time to whirl around, I could hear the *clip-clop, clip-clop* of hooves approaching.

I quickly got into position; my heart began to race as I realized I'd only have one chance to get this right. One mistake and the armed guards would easily kill me. I glanced back at the approaching carriage once more and realized that I needed to move a few feet to the left or I'd miss it entirely. It was hard to make myself tiptoe briskly across the limb, but I made myself do it and managed to keep hidden all at the same time.

Two horses, side by side, trotted under me, immediately followed by the two guards seated on a red leather cushion. I reached outward for a sturdy, low-hanging branch a few feet in front of me and then carefully swung forward, landing quietly onto the roof of the prison carriage as it rolled beneath me.

Just as I crouched down, the carriage began to slow. Glancing ahead, I noticed a drunken, filthy man stumble into the dusty road. The carriage came to an abrupt halt.

"Get out of the way, you blundering fool," one of the guards commanded harshly.

The blundering fool he was referring to was Gordon, of course.

Gordon slurred an incoherent response, raised his fist at the guards in defiance, and then passed out on the road; an empty bottle of rum fell from his hand and spun into the middle of the road. The other guard seemed amused and began to chuckle. The first guard spoke again and his tone remained harsh. Although he seemed to believe Gordon's performance was authentic, it was clear he found no humor in it.

"I said get out of the way, fool!" he said again.

Gordon remained still.

"If you don't get out of the way, I'll throw you in the back of this carriage," he barked. "You'll hang right nicely with all the other scum."

"Albert, can't you see the bloody man is passed out?" The other guard asked, a bit of pity in his voice. "Come along and help me get him out of the way."

"Are you mad? He smells like horse dung!"

"Well, either we move him or we run him over."

"Then it's settled, we run him over," Albert quipped.

The other guard stifled a chuckle but thankfully stayed diligent. "Come along, let's get this over with," he said.

He began to rise from his seat; Albert sighed deeply but reluctantly did the same. As soon as they were both standing, they instantly froze as they heard me pull back both hammers on my pistols.

"Put both of your grubby paws up, very slowly," I ordered in a stern voice. They both obliged, but Albert started to turn around to face me. "Albert, I'd keep that nose pointed east, mate—unless of course you'd like to lose it."

"You'll hang for this," he replied through clenched teeth.

"Gentlemen, no one is hanging tonight," Gordon, now on his feet and holding a blunderbuss, replied. "Throw any weapons you've got onto the street." Both guards glanced silently at each other. It was obvious they were contemplating trying something stupid. "You only get one warning," Gordon stated, reading their thoughts. There was another moment of hesitation. Gordon pulled back the hammer on the blunderbuss. This time the guards hurriedly threw pistols and swords onto the street.

"I want both of you to slowly exit the carriage," I commanded. This time there was no verbal response from Albert. Both guards did as they were told.

"Walk into the graveyard," Gordon ordered and again they did as they were told.

He then snatched a ring of keys off a loop on Albert's pants and tossed it to me. I made my way down onto the carriage's red cushioned seat and just as I was about to grab a side rail and swing around to release Andy Bonnet, our plan began to unravel. I noticed a redcoat on horseback rounding the corner at Tower Street. As soon as I saw him, I froze, hoping deep down that if I was still enough and quiet enough he wouldn't see me. For a brief moment, it seemed that my silent prayers would work. He didn't even give me a passing glance and prepared to turn toward York Street. But then Albert noticed him too.

"Jail break!" he barked. "Jail break!"

The red coat turned toward us and immediately realized what was happening. He held two fingers to his mouth and whistled loudly. I could hear at least two more horses galloping from somewhere out of view, probably further down York Street.

I glanced in Gordon's direction but there was no need for me to beckon him. He was already climbing on board the carriage.

"Quickly, grab the reigns!"

As soon as Gordon had the carriage moving, I grabbed the side rail and swung around to unlock the prison door. I took a quick glance behind us and saw what I expected. Three red coats were thundering toward us, their horses in full sprint. I forced myself to look away and put my focus back on the key ring. There were at least ten different keys to choose from on the ring. I estimated that I only had enough time to try about three of them before the red coats caught up to us. I jabbed the first key into the hole… it didn't work. I tried another key with the same frustrating result. A pair of shackled hands suddenly poked out from between the bars of the door's window. I peered into the carriage and realized the hands belonged to Andy Bonnett. His head was covered with a black bag, and I could hear him speak, but the sound was so muffled I was unable to understand what he was saying. I thrust the ring of keys into his hands.

"Here mate," I shouted. "Get your shackles off and then work on getting this door open. I've got bigger problems right now."

Apparently, Andy understood because he wasted no time yanking the keys into the carriage with him.

There was a sudden thunderous *boom* from the road behind us followed immediately by a *clang* and a spark of light off the handrail I was holding onto. The shot had been fired from the soldier nearest to me, but fortunately his aim was off.

For lack of a better term, it scared the hell out of me. I involuntarily let go of the rail for a brief instant, but it was a long enough moment to almost kill me. I fell toward the ground but managed to grab one of the metal steps below the door on the way down. I hung on to the steps as if my life depended on it, and because my legs were now being dragged dangerously close to the rear wheels of the carriage, my life really *did* depend on it. I started to pull myself back up, but immediately stopped when I noticed a horse galloping a few feet away from me. I glanced up at the rider and was greeted with a pistol pointed toward my head. I was a sitting duck. There was nothing I could do but close my eyes and wait on my imminent death.

I heard a loud explosion, but the death I expected never came. I opened my eyes and saw my attacker rolling across the dusty street behind us. His now rider-less horse veered away and disappeared onto another street. I looked up and was surprised to see Gordon peering down at me from around the front corner of the carriage, the blunderbuss smoking in his right hand. I gave him a nod of gratitude and then immediately went back to work pulling myself up. I knew there were two more soldiers on horseback approaching and if I was going to have any chance of dealing with them I had to get back on my feet.

The carriage door suddenly swung open and a helping hand appeared in my line of sight. Without hesitation, I took Andy's hand—his tiny, boyish hand—and after a few moments of exertion I found myself lying on the inside of the prison carriage, at least temporarily safe from our pursuers. I got my first look at Andy and although the wide-brimmed hat he was wearing obscured some of his face, it was still plain to see he was only a lad, no more than seventeen or eighteen at the most.

"Are you alright, sir?" he asked me, very politely.

"I am, lad, thanks a lot for the help." I tossed him one of my pistols and some shot. "Reload and get ready, this may get a bit nasty," I told him as I prepared my own weapon.

"We're approaching the court house!" Gordon yelled from outside. "We need to get in position!"

"Be right there!" I shouted back to him. Andy had just rammed a ball down the barrel of his pistol when I grabbed his arm. He looked up at me, wide-eyed with fear etched all over his dirty face. "Andy, have you ever shot a man?"

He said nothing, but shook his head side to side.

Wonderful, I thought. It was starting to make sense why Captain Trimble marooned the pathetic lad.

I poked my head out the door to get a quick glance of the redcoats chasing us. Two horses were side by side and only a few feet behind us. They were certainly capable of pulling alongside us; however, the unknown plotting that was going on inside the carriage seemed to encourage a cautious pursuit for the moment. The blunderbuss Gordon had used to dispose of one of their fellow soldiers was obviously still fresh on their minds as well. One of them spotted me peeking and began to shout furious curses at me. I was unable to resist the urge to quickly stick my tongue out at him in reply. I didn't wait for a response and pulled my head back in to safety. Andy stared at me, awaiting instructions.

"Andy, all I need you to do is follow me to the roof of the carriage. I don't really care how you do it. You've got a pistol; use the shot wisely," I said. He stared at me, obviously unsure if he was up to the task. "Please, Andy," I pleaded. "We have to get to the roof if we're going to escape tonight."

He seemed to straighten and nodded. The weight of the situation was apparently sinking in. He could either do what I said, or he was going to die.

I moved toward the door again but paused as an idea came to mind. I looked over at Andy, and then down at his feet.

"What?" he asked fearfully.

"Give me one of your shoes," I replied.

He squinted at me, opened his mouth to speak, but thought better of it. He then reached down and handed me his right shoe without further hesitation. I took the shoe by the toe and slowly thrust it out the door.

As expected, a loud explosion was heard and the shoe jerked out of my grasp when the shot hit it.

"There, I just made them waste one shot," I shouted as I darted out the door. "Please move quickly!" I grabbed the side rail and frantically pulled and clawed my way to the roof of the carriage. Another thunderous blast rang out. The proximity of the sound immediately told me it originated from Andy. I took a quick glance to the rear of the carriage and saw another red coat rolling across High Street. I allowed myself a brief smile, and then pulled my own pistol out. I planned on disposing of the remaining soldier, but unfortunately, he wasn't in my line of sight. Andy's hand slapped at the roof; he was trying to find something to grab on to. I returned the pistol to its holster and grabbed the far side of the carriage with my right hand. I grabbed Andy's hand with my left and pulled him up with all the strength I could muster. He was lighter than I anticipated, but my shoulder still burned with pain as I pulled. He finally managed to get a leg up on to the roof and rolled on top of me. Gordon still had the carriage moving at a fast pace, and it was obvious Andy had not taken the time to tighten his hat snugly on his head as I had done earlier. The wind promptly blew the wide-brimmed hat off his head and I finally could see all of Andy's face. I have no idea for sure how my expression looked, but there was no doubt my jaw dropped open at what I saw. Andy winced as the hat blew away.

"Why didn't you tell me?" I shouted.

"I'm sorry, but I just bloody met you!" Andy shouted back.

"Captain, will you please hurry the hell up!" Gordon shouted from the front seat. "We're going downhill and we've almost reached the cliffs!"

I shook my head in disbelief once more, and then glared at Andy again. "I'll deal with this later," I barked. "You stay down as low as you can right here."

Andy said nothing but rolled off me and laid as flat as humanly possible in response. I crawled to the front of the carriage and slid down into the seat beside Gordon.

"There's one more redcoat back there," I said. "Keep the horses headed straight and true. I'll take care of the harness."

I hung my body off the front of the carriage and suddenly felt that I was in the most danger I'd been in the entire night. I could literally feel the power of the horses in front of me as they kicked up dirt and other debris in my face as they galloped at full speed. I hadn't anticipated this, and it was hard enough to see in the dark without having dirt kicked in my face too. I retrieved a knife from my belt and then carefully placed the hilt into my mouth. I bit down hard to ensure I didn't drop it and then began reaching frantically for the traces connecting the horse's harnesses to the carriage. My hand finally found the chains and I felt my way along the cool metal links until I felt the connecting leather straps. I wasted no time slicing through the straps, which in turn released the horses.

"Gordon, release the reigns!"

He did as I commanded. The horses were apparently aware of their impending doom because they wasted no time veering off our current heading and disappeared into the darkness. Now the only thing ahead of us was a few hundred feet of earth that ended abruptly with at least a five hundred foot drop into the Atlantic Ocean.

I quickly climbed back into the seat and followed Gordon who was already pulling his body up on the roof. Once we were both on the roof, Gordon glanced at Andy, did a double take, and then glanced at me.

"Who the bloody hell is this?" he shouted.

"Andy Bonnet of course," I answered.

"Actually, my name is Andrea," Andy corrected us. "How do you do?" she asked nonchalantly, her long blonde hair flowing wildly in the wind.

The look of confusion on Gordon's face no doubt matched my own, but this was no time to discuss the fact that Andy—Andrea— was in fact a woman. I refocused my attention on the vast openness beyond the cliffs ahead. The carriage seemed to be picking up speed as it progressed down the hill.

"Okay, this is it," I yelled. "As soon as the carriage goes off the cliff, jump off and get as far away from it as you can. We don't want this thing crashing on top of us and trapping us under the water."

Gordon nodded as he knew what to expect, Andrea on the other hand had a look of complete terror wash over her dirty face.

"Are you sure about this?" she screamed.

"No, of course not," I answered.

For a moment it seemed her fear subsided and was replaced by anger. However, that moment was short lived as the prison carriage launched off the cliff like it had been fired from a twelve-pounder.

The ground beneath us disappeared and was replaced immediately with a large canvas of ocean. We managed to push our bodies away from the falling block of iron on wheels, and the fall seemed to take minutes rather than seconds. I must confess that I expected to hear Andrea screaming on the way down, and maybe she was, but I would never have been able to hear it over Gordon's own high-pitched wailing.

I finally contacted the water, feet first, and my body tore through the sea as smoothly as an arrow. I plunged so far down I half expected my boots to hit the sandy bottom at any second. When the sensation of earth under my feet never came, I made my way back to the surface in a much slower fashion than I'd experienced on the way down. It was an eerie feeling, swimming in total blackness, and for a moment it occurred to me that there was no way to be certain if I was even swimming up or down. I allowed my instincts to guide me and when I finally did burst through the wall of water and back into the cool night air, my attention immediately turned toward finding Gordon and Andrea.

"Gordon!" I shouted. "Andrea, are you there?"

I heard a gurgling, followed by an odd splashing sound. I looked behind me just in time to see the rear corner of the prison carriage disappear beneath the calm waters.

"Sir," I heard Andrea shout. "Sir, I'm over here!"

I saw her treading water even further out than where I'd seen the carriage sink. As I swam toward her I looked both directions for any sign of Gordon. I didn't see or hear any sign of him and just as I was beginning to worry I heard another voice that wasn't Gordon's.

"That was a hell of a ride, Cap'n," Langley called out from somewhere to my right. My eyes finally adjusted enough to the darkness to make out the silhouette of a small rowboat drifting toward Andrea.

"Yes, it was quite fun actually," I replied.

Langley had come through for me, just as he always did. Gordon doubted him, but I did not. The thought brought on the realization that I still had not located Gordon. I did my best to quell the spark of panic that was trying desperately to ignite.

"Langley, have you seen Gordon?"

"I've got him, Cap'n. He's a lucky swab, he is. He was knocked out cold when I found him floating on the surface. Probably popped his head on that carriage."

I was somewhat alarmed at this news, but at the same time Langley's tone didn't sound very concerned. This eased my mind a little as I swam to the boat. Langley was pulling Andrea on board as I pulled myself on board behind him. I crawled toward Gordon and quickly put my ear to his chest. There was a heartbeat and his chest moved up and down... he was breathing. I turned my attention to his head and I found a nice lump just above his right eyebrow at the hairline. There was a small cut as well, but little blood to speak of. Langley was right; he was indeed a lucky man tonight.

"Langley, to the cave... quickly!"

"Who are you gentlemen?" Andrea asked suddenly.

I turned to face her and figured now was as good a time as any to tell her.

"My dear, the man who is currently napping is Gordon Littleton. Our rescuer there is Oliver Langley. I am the notorious Captain Redd Reeves," I said gleefully.

There was no mistaking her puzzled expression, even in the darkness. "You're who?"

I snorted and was unsure as to whether I should be offended or embarrassed.

"You seriously have never heard of me?"

She shook her head. "I'm sorry."

I rolled my eyes, fully aware of the fact she'd be unable to see it. "I suppose it doesn't matter right now dear. What does matter is this: were you or were you not recently among the crew of Captain Winston Trimble?"

There was a long silence, and all that could be heard was the subtle splashing that resulted from Langley's steady rowing.

"Captain Trimble marooned me... left me for dead," she said finally. Her tone suggested that she was genuinely hurt by what Trimble had done to her. I knew she was young, but I found it difficult to understand how she did not realize how incredibly lucky she was to have not suffered a worse fate at the hands of such a sadistic mad man.

"Andrea, marooning a man—or in your case a woman—is a terrible fate for any pirate. But frankly I'm surprised Trimble let you off so easy."

She said nothing in response.

"What I'd really like to know," I continued, "is how a young lass like yourself ended up aboard a bloody pirate ship. And not just any pirate ship… you wound up on the most feared pirate ship of the entire world. Tell me, how does that happen, dearie?"

I could hear her sniffling and it suddenly became apparent that the woman was crying. I was taken aback; I didn't know what to say. How did a woman like Andrea become a pirate? She clearly didn't have the stomach for it.

"The way it happens," she began through the sobs. "The way it happened to me is… Captain Trimble is my father," she said abruptly. Andrea then planted her face in her hands and the tears flowed aplenty.

Chapter 4

The sea seemed as much a part of Oliver Langley as his arms and legs. He could guide a ship (or in this case a rowboat) through the darkness with as much precision as he could through the brightest of days. As strange as it sounds, the instincts that seemed to guide him were even sharper after he'd drank a few pints of rum. It was hard for me to see anything in the moonless summer night, and all I could do was trust Langley to get us to our destination with enough haste to evade the inevitable swarm of red coats that would soon begin searching the water for survivors.

I wondered if they would be smart enough to realize that our dangerous escape was all part of a well-executed plan. Obviously, it was my hope that they would believe it was an escape plot that went terribly wrong. There would no doubt be confusion early on, but I knew as soon as they examined the cut leather straps that had once connected the horses to the carriage, it would become apparent that they were dealing with a daring escape plan instead of a foiled one.

Time was critical. Getting out of the water without a trace would be vital to our success. There was one more player in our eventful night that was awaiting our arrival in a tiny, hidden cave just below the rocky cliff from which the Parrot's Landing rested, overlooking the bay.

The opening was barely large enough for the boat to slip through, but Langley guided the little vessel into the cave with ease on the first attempt. After the boat traveled another thirty feet, the cave suddenly opened into a much larger chamber. The jagged ceiling was low, but the stone walls were far apart.

A short and frail silver-haired man stood on a rocky ledge at the far end of the chamber. He was holding a torch and watching us with a posture that suggested he was extremely tired. Seeing him that way made me feel a pang of guilt. The man had to be pushing seventy, and here I was keeping him out of bed in the late hours of the night.

Tired as he was, John Copperton was exactly where he promised me he'd be when he, Gordon Littleton, Oliver Langley, and I worked out our plan in a back room of the Parrot's Landing a couple of hours earlier.

John owned the Parrot's Landing, and although he had a good reputation among Port Royal's government, he was secretly known to be an ally to pirates everywhere. A trap door existed under a rug in the stock room of his establishment, and underneath that door was a secret passageway that twisted and turned through the rocky earth and ended in the chamber we now found ourselves in. John was reluctant to assist us with such a risky endeavor, but the man was practically family to me. There was no way he could tell me no.

Langley eased the boat back to its rightful place. I briskly stepped out of the boat and onto the rocky ledge. Langley tossed a coiled rope my way; I caught it and immediately tied the line around a large, rusty spike that had been driven into the stone ledge many, many years earlier.

"William, you're going to be the death of me," John said when I turned to face him. I smiled at him.

John Copperton was probably the only man besides Gordon that could call me William without me taking a swing at him. The man had been the closest thing to a father figure I'd had since my real father was murdered when I was a young lad living in London.

My father... I hadn't thought of my real flesh-and-blood father in years. The revelation suddenly unleashed a flood of memories of the hellish childhood that molded me into the man I was today...

My mother died shortly after I was born. Her death apparently affected my father in a pretty significant way because he began to drink heavily. I've been told that prior to my mother's untimely death, he had a very decent job as a store clerk, but he was soon fired because he was never sober enough to work.

The combination of my mother's death, loss of income, and booze completely changed my father's outlook on life and eventually led him to a life of crime. My father must have been a successful thief because he and I never starved. I remembered many occasions when my father would leave me home alone when I was as young as four. He may have left me alone at a younger age than that, but I have no way to know for sure since my memories do not go back that far.

Ten years passed swiftly and it seemed that, as unusual and unorthodox as our life had become, my father and I were going to somehow make it through our hardships and live happily ever after.

It wasn't meant to be.

Unfortunately, my father also developed a gambling problem that later led to a significantly large unpaid debt. On a snowy Christmas Eve in the year 1699, there was a knock on the door. My father was usually a very cautious man due to his line of work, but on this particular night he made no attempt to peek through a nearby window to see who was on the doorstep. He opened the door without a care in the world, and a man by the name of Charles Higgins promptly slit his throat with a barber's razor before my father even had a chance to scream.

He fell like a sack of potatoes, and after a brief spell of wild thrashing on the floor, he was gone. I was only a boy of ten and seeing that much blood on the floor was utterly shocking. I stood there staring at my dead father, my mouth hung open as if I was in some sort of trance, and I guess it's fair to say that I was, in a sense.

A look of horror washed across Mr. Higgins's face when he spotted me. I don't think he had any idea at the time that my father even had a son. All he knew was that the dead man at his feet owed him a large debt, and the man had paid for it with his life. I'm not sure it would've even made a difference in the long run if he'd known I was his son.

At that time, however, it *did* seem to make a difference to him because the look of horror was suddenly replaced by a somber expression of pity as he looked down on me.

He stepped toward me and for a moment I feared that he was going to kill me too, but instead he scooped me up and carried me out of my home and into the bitter cold night. Higgins moved swiftly and discreetly through the dark alleys of London with me upon his shoulder. We eventually emerged at a dock and before I knew it I found myself on the deck of a large ship, the largest I'd ever seen at the time. I don't know why, but somehow, I knew immediately that I was on board a pirate ship. On an ordinary night, this realization would've undoubtedly terrified me. However, this was no ordinary night. My father had just been murdered and his death, along with the vision of all that blood on the floor, was still fresh in my mind.

Higgins stopped at the captain's cabin and began pounding frantically on the door. After a long moment, the door opened and a wrinkled and weathered face peered out. The captain had a large nose with a large, bushy mustache that curved down sharply and disappeared into a gray beard that enveloped the lower half of his face. His eyes were tired but attentive. The captain seemed to know that there must have been a good reason for one of his officers to wake him at such an unusual hour.

His boatswain, Higgins, began to tell the tale of what had happened on my father's doorstep earlier in the night. He spoke so fast that I wasn't sure if the pirate captain could comprehend a word that spilled from his chapped lips. When he finally finished, the old captain looked down at meet, pity and sorrow etched in the deep lines of his face. He then knelt to my level and peered sharply into my eyes. The shadows of the night darkened half of his face and I could smell the strong scent of rum on his breath. He asked me my name and I told him, my voice soft and fearful. The old captain proceeded to tell me very matter-of-factly that given my current predicament, there were only two possible outcomes and the choice was completely mine to make. My first option was death. There was no hesitation in his voice when he told me. It was made very clear to me that if I did not choose the second option, I would be killed. I was promised that the death would be quick and almost painless.

The second option given was an opportunity to sign the articles and join the crew of his ship. As a ten-year-old boy, this option was not very appealing to me, especially since I'd probably see my father's killer on a daily basis. However, the fear of dying made the decision easier and minutes later I found myself in the captain's cabin signing my life away...

"William, are you alright?" John asked, snatching me back to the present.

I shook my head and nodded.

"I'm fine," I said. "Thanks again. I couldn't have pulled this off without you."

He waved off my thanks and I noticed him eyeing Andrea. He shot a look of confusion my way.

"This is Andrea Bonnett," I said. "She's the prisoner we helped escape."

"As you say," he replied, still staring at her.

Andrea glanced at me, obviously uncomfortable with the awkward staring. "Does he always stare at new acquaintances like this?"

Her words seem to snap him out of his trance and his face suddenly flushed a nice shade of pink.

"Oh, I'm truly sorry, Miss... you're just not what I was expecting, is all," John stammered. "You don't look the least bit like any pirate I've ever seen, and I've seen a lot of pirates over the years."

Andrea smiled at him, suddenly understanding his bewildered state.

"I'm not so sure you've seen all that many pirates then," she replied. "Lady pirates are much more common than you think."

"Aye, I've met my share of woman pirates," John said. "However, the woman pirates I've met over the years are less..." He seemed to struggle to find the right word.

"Less what?" she asked.

"Less... less..."

"Beautiful," I interrupted. "Less beautiful, it's okay to say it John. She is indeed quite beautiful."

John's face turned a shade of pink yet again, and Andrea's did the same.

"What are you three bunglers raving on about?" Langley asked suddenly. "Cap'n, I could sure use a hand with Gordon."

I hurried over to the boat and grabbed Gordon's legs; Langley had him under the arms. He was still unconscious and all dead weight.

John led the way up the stone-carved stairs, torch in hand, followed by Andrea. When we finally arrived in the stock room, John rolled up a thick overcoat and we lay Gordon down, his head resting on the wool coat.

"We're going to have to leave him here for the night," I said. "We can't move him through the streets without drawing suspicion."

"None of you will be able to go out there without drawing suspicion," John said. "You're *all* going to have to stay here for the night."

"No, we can't risk that," I said. "They're going to still be searching in the morning and the streets will probably be even more buttoned up than they are right now."

John squinted and scratched his head. He always did that when he was deep in thought. Suddenly, his face lit up.

"I think I've got an idea to get you all to your ship unnoticed," he said. He glanced at Andrea. "But I'm sorry to say it won't be all that pleasant, Miss."

"I can handle whatever you have in mind if it leads to my freedom," she answered without hesitation.

"Very well," he replied. "Follow me."

Andrea, Langley, and I followed him to the furthest corner of the stock room. There was a rather large stack of wooden crates and barrels arranged neatly in the corner.

"When the merchants I use bring me a new shipment of goods, they usually ask that I send back the empty containers when I'm through with them. This is where I keep them all until they return. As you can see, some of them are quite large. Some are so large you could fit a couple of pirates in them."

He glanced at me and I soon realized what he was thinking.

"You know," I said, smiling. "The sloop that the governor has provided me is still in need of supplies."

"I don't mind making a late-night delivery," John said.

Langley grumbled as he realized what was about to happen. "Cap'n, let's bustle to it. I'm not getting any younger and my old bones can't take this sort of abuse for very long."

I clasped a hand on his shoulder.

"I think we'll stow you away in your own rum barrel, Langley. The sweet aroma will make the trip somewhat easier."

"Aye, it may," he replied. "Let's get on with it."

"I suppose we can give the lady her own barrel as well," said John.

"That won't be necessary," she replied. "I will share a crate with Captain Redd. Give Mr. Littleton his own barrel, he is injured and should be handled carefully."

I was briefly taken aback when I heard that she wanted to share a crate with me. "Andrea, are you sure you wouldn't like your own—"

"Captain, I will be just fine sharing a crate," she snapped. "Unless, of course, you are unwilling to share one with me."

She stared at me with sparkling sky blue eyes and awaited my response.

"It's settled then," I said. "Langley and Gordon will ride separately in their own barrels. Andrea and I will share a crate."

"Very well," said John, reaching for a barrel. "Let's hurry; time is precious."

With the help of one of John's most trusted employees, we were sealed in our containers and placed onto the back of a covered wagon in less than half an hour. The crate Andrea and I were in was large enough for us to face each other. We had our arms clasped around our legs and knees pressed against our chests. There was still a foot between us. I removed my hat and it provided me enough room to move my head freely. I knew we were finally on our way when the wagon lurched forward.

"Why did you rescue me?" Andrea asked abruptly from the pitch-black darkness.

It soon became apparent to me why she'd wanted to share a crate. She had lots of questions. That was okay though because I had my share of questions too.

"I'm trying to find Captain Trimble," I answered. "I saved you from the gallows in hopes that you'd be able to provide me some sort of heading."

"Why are you trying to find my father?" she asked in a tone that had a subtle hint of anger attached to it. Whether it was directed at me, or her father, was a mystery.

"He's got something that I want—a ring."

There was a long silence. The quiet seemed to suggest that Andrea knew exactly what I was talking about.

"Do you know of the ring I'm speaking of?"

"Yes, I know of King Solomon's ring," she replied. "What do you want with it?"

"I hear that the ring has extraordinary powers. A man like Captain Trimble shouldn't have that sort of power."

Another long silence passed; then I heard a soft chuckle.

"Is something funny?" I asked.

"You're a bloody privateer, aren't you?" she said, more anger in her voice. This time I knew it was directed at me. "The king hired you to get the ring back, didn't he?"

There was no use in denying it.

"Something like that," I answered. "But let's be clear on this: I am no privateer. I was told to retrieve that ring in exchange for my freedom."

"If you're working under the king's authority, you *are* a privateer," she said.

The wagon suddenly jolted hard and I felt the uncomfortable sensation of the crate bouncing into the air. My head struck the wooden lid.

Damn potholes, I thought.

"Okay, I'm a privateer then," I conceded out of sheer annoyance. I rubbed my aching skull. "Can you help me find your father or not?"

"Let's assume that I do know where my father is. Just what do you plan on doing when we find him?"

At that moment, I was very glad Andrea was unable to see me in the darkness of the crate. There was probably a look of sheer stupidity on my face. I really had no idea what I was going to do to stop a man with that sort of power at his disposal. Reluctantly, I remained honest with her.

"I honestly haven't thought that far ahead," I replied sheepishly.

Andrea began laughing wildly. The cackle that erupted from her lips was almost scary and for a moment, in the darkness, she seemed exactly what one would imagine the daughter of Captain Winston Trimble to be.

"That's what I thought you were going to say," she said, snorting through laughter. "There can only be two reasons you would go after my father so blindly. Either you're the bravest pirate that ever lived, or the stupidest one. Tell me, Captain Redd, which one are you?"

I bit my lip to refrain from saying something I would regret. I needed Andrea's help and now she knew it. As angry as I was, I held back the barrage of curses begging me to unleash them.

"Andrea," I said with disciplined grace. "Do you know where your father is or not?"

She sighed and pondered the question for a moment before she spoke.

"I do not," she said finally. "But I know where to find men that will probably be able to give us a heading."

"Well, that's wonderful," I said with relief. "Where do we find them?"

"New Providence is teeming with pirate captains who knew my father and…" Her words trailed off as if something had just occurred to her. "I have an idea," she said suddenly.

"Let's hear it then."

"If you're going to get that ring from my father, you're going to need a bargaining chip," she said.

My eyebrows arched. It seemed now we were finally making progress. "Go on."

"There is an old man that lives in New Providence. He will most likely have a rough idea on my father's whereabouts," she said. "He is also probably the only man alive that knows where my father buried a chest containing his most important possession."

"A chest," I said, suddenly more interested. "A chest containing *what* important possession?"

"I do not know exactly what is in the chest," she admitted. "But I know that whatever it is, my father has gone to great lengths to keep its location hidden. If we could find it, it may be just what we need to bargain with him."

My mind began to flood with thoughts of what could be in such a chest. Was it gold? Jewels? Or could it be something more sinister?

"Okay," I said. "That sounds like a wonderful plan, but why do you think that this man would give up the location of the chest to us?"

"He will give up the location to *me*," she corrected. "And he'll do it because he is my uncle. If I tell him that my father is in danger and is in need of the chest… well, it just might be enough."

"Are you saying this old man is Captain Trimble's brother?"

"Yes, his elder brother," she replied. "His name is Morgan Trimble. Have you ever heard of him?"

"No, I don't think so," I said.

"He sailed under Captain Kidd on the *Adventure Prize* in the late 1600s. He was a fearsome pirate, one of the few who escaped before Kidd was arrested. His age is what finally did him in. He gave up that life—well, to a point anyway," she said. "I mean, he *did* choose to live out his final days in a pirate haven."

"Alright, as soon as the sloop is ready to go we'll set sail for New Providence," I said.

The wagon suddenly came to an abrupt halt.

"Finally," I grumbled. "My knees are beginning to ache."

Unfortunately, it suddenly became apparent that we had not arrived at the ship as I had hoped. I could hear talking near the front of the wagon, but it was too muffled to make out what was being said.

"Soldiers have stopped the wagon," Andrea said suddenly.

"Can you hear them?" I asked.

"Yes, they're asking Mr. Copperton about his cargo."

"What is he saying?" I asked, frustrated that she could hear and I could not.

"He's telling them that he's headed for the docks with it," she replied. "The soldiers are telling him that they are searching for an escaped fugitive and they need to search the wagon."

"That's just wonderful," I whispered through clenched teeth. I grabbed my pistol and drew back the hammer.

Andrea heard the gun *click* as I readied the weapon.

"Are you mad?" she hissed. "We don't even know how many soldiers are out there!"

"I'm just getting prepared," I replied. "John is a clever man. I'm betting he'll find a way out of this."

The soldiers made their way to the back of the wagon and suddenly I could hear them quite well. Unfortunately, I realized that this meant they would be able to hear us easily as well.

"What are the contents of the containers?" I heard a man's commanding voice call out.

"I already told you. There is cider, sugar, spices and a mixture of fruits and vegetables," John replied firmly.

There was a brief silence and I could hear someone climb up into the wagon.

"Mr. Copperton," the soldier continued. "Would you mind if we check the contents for ourselves?"

"As a matter of fact, I would," John replied angrily. "Are you suggesting that I am lying, sir?"

"We are merely being thorough," the soldier countered. "It would be wise of you to stay out of the way."

I cringed as I heard the soldier speak the words. It was clear that he didn't know John Copperton very well.

"Sir, do you have any idea who I am?" John asked.

"Mr. Copperton, I must confess I do not and that is precisely why I want to search your wagon," the soldier replied, agitated. "You, sir, are apparently unaware of who I am as well. I'm here under the authority of Governor Winters and you would—"

"I am a close acquaintance of the governor!" John snarled. "I will be sure to tell him how I was treated tonight as soon as the sun comes up."

The soldier seemed unaffected by the threat.

"Mr. Copperton, I am going to ask you once more to voluntarily let me verify that the fugitive isn't in this wagon and if you refuse I will do so by force."

"And I'm going to warn you one more time to get back on your horse and leave me be, laddie," John growled.

"Very well, have it your way," the soldier said.

I could clearly make out the sound of metal sliding from leather.

"Put that pistol away at once!" John shouted.

My heart rate picked up, and it took all the restraint I could muster to keep from bursting from the crate. The feeling of helplessness I'd felt hours earlier when I was in shackles suddenly crept back into mind. Andrea was deadly quiet. There was virtually nothing either of us could do. Suddenly, a thunderous *boom* tore through the night air.

Why was this man firing his bloody weapon? Had he shot John?

There was a brief moment of silence before I got my answer.

"Well, I hope you're satisfied," John huffed. "You put a nice round hole in a perfectly good barrel of cider."

Now I could make out the sound of liquid chugging swiftly from a barrel and spattering all over the road beneath the wagon. Fortunately, it seemed the soldier chose a barrel to shoot that did not contain Gordon or Langley. I held my breath and hoped it was enough for them to let John go.

"Mr. Copperton," the soldier said. "I thank you for your cooperation, you may move along."

"Governor Winters will hear about this, young man," John said. "You will pay for the barrel of cider you just ruined."

The soldier kept his calm demeanor and again ignored the threat.

"Mr. Copperton, if you see or hear anything regarding the escaped prisoner, I trust you will tell the authorities immediately" was the reply.

Moments later the rhythmic sound of multiple horses galloping away was followed by a loud sigh of relief from Andrea.

"*That* was too close," she said.

"Aye, it certainly was," I replied.

John returned to the front of the wagon and we were moving again. The rest of the short trip was uninterrupted. When we arrived at the docks, John had two of his men transport all the barrels and crates below the deck of the sloop Governor Winters had promised me. It was only then that we were safe enough to come out of hiding. Once I was out, I stood and stretched my arms. We had been bottled up a lot longer than we'd planned.

I peered over at Langley. The lantern that hung overhead wasn't very bright, but it provided just enough light for me to make him out. He was seated on a water cask and massaging both knees.

"That's something I'd rather not do ever again, Cap'n," he said.

"Me either." I turned to John. "You handled those soldiers beautifully."

"Did I?" he asked wearily. "I'm not so sure. That young pup could've easily put a shot into one of you three, and there would have been nothing I could've done to stop it."

"You did well," Andrea assured him. "We're all here alive. That's the important thing." She leaned toward him and kissed him on the cheek. "Thank you, John."

It was a shame that the light was so dim; I would've enjoyed seeing the old man's face.

"It was my pleasure, lass," he replied. I could hear the delight in his voice. He suddenly didn't sound so weary anymore. "Oh! I almost forgot."

He pulled a cloth sack from a nearby crate and tossed it to Andrea.

"Seeing how you're now a fugitive, it's probably a good idea for you to change clothes," he said. "They're men's clothing and they may be a bit baggy, but they'll do the job."

She took the bag and hugged John graciously.

"Thank you again, kind sir," she said.

After the embrace, John let out a tired sigh. He was looking more exhausted by the minute.

"I'm afraid I must be going now," he said wearily. "Good luck to the lot of you."

I reached for John and hugged him tightly. He stuck his neck out for me yet again. I told myself that this would surely be the last time.

"Thank you, John. You've never let me down."

"You know I'm always here for you, boy," he replied.

It was a tender moment, one of the few in my life. He bid us all good luck, and then he was gone.

Chapter 5

Oliver Langley wasted no time collapsing into the first hammock he happened upon in the crew's quarters of the ship. I'd already decided that the best place for both Gordon and Andrea would be in my quarters. It was essential that Gordon recover from his injury as soon as possible, and it seemed to me that the best place for him would be on a soft bed. As it happened, the only soft bed found on the ship was in the captain's quarters.

I threw Gordon upon my shoulder and quickly made my way across the deck with Andrea on my heels. I barged through the door of the captain's quarters and casually dropped Gordon's limp body into bed. It was very dark, but there was no need to light a lantern. I found Andrea a cot and minutes after she lay down, I could hear the heavy, rhythmic breathing of her sleeping. I stood there a moment with my hands upon my sides and reflected on the events of the day.

It was truly miraculous that I was still alive!

I thought of the sloop I now found myself in. I knew very little about her and had not even seen how she looked from the outside. I would have to get acquainted with the ship very quickly in the morning if I was going to be able to set sail by early afternoon.

Exhaustion weighed heavily on my eyelids and I considered options for my own sleeping arrangement. Tired as I was, I simply grabbed a wooden chair from a nearby table, sat down, and leaned it carefully back against the wall. I lowered the tricorn hat down over my eyes and finally drifted off to sleep.

The next morning I was awakened suddenly by the moaning and groaning of Gordon Littleton. The sound startled me, and I came very close to tipping my chair over. Gordon was still lying in the bed, but he was massaging his temples.

I took the groaning and the movement as a good sign.

"As soon as I get a little rum and porridge in you, you'll be good as new," I muttered.

"I'm afraid it's going to be quite a while before I'm good as new," he groaned.

Gordon arose from the bed in a gingerly fashion, allowing both legs to swing lazily off the bed and onto the floor. He stood for a moment and I could tell he was considering whether he should try and walk. There was a glazed-over look in his eyes; he almost seemed drunk.

"Sit down, you crass fool," I commanded. "You'll end up falling and cracking that skull of yours open the rest of the way."

I walked over and gently pushed him back down on to the bed. He scowled at me but remained seated. Andrea stirred on the cot in the corner; she'd apparently been listening to our exchange.

"The captain is right," she said. "You should sit down, Gordon."

"I'll remain seated if you'll find something for my belly," he replied. "It's past time for breakfast, and I'm not going to be very useful at all on an empty stomach."

Andrea stood and stretched.

"I think we can manage that," she said and then looked at me. "Right, Captain?"

I wasn't very comfortable leaving Gordon alone. He was a stubborn man and often disobeyed any orders regarding his personal well-being. It wouldn't surprise me at all if he jumped up and started getting his navigational charts together the minute that we left the ship.

On the other hand, I needed some time alone with Andrea to discuss a few things regarding Captain Trimble and the signet ring of King Solomon. I decided to leave him alone and if he fell and cracked his bloody skull while we were away, it would be his own cursed fault.

"Gordon, you stay right there until we get back. Agreed?"

His response was exactly as I expected.

"Sure, Captain, I'll be right here when you return. I like my eggs scrambled, if you please."

I rolled my eyes and motioned for Andrea to follow me. When we were outside and on deck, I was surprised to already see several members of my crew on board. They were sprawled all about the deck, their bellies no doubt full of rum. Many of them were still sleeping off the wild night before. I figured this was as good a time as any to get things back to normalcy.

"Up with you!" I shouted. "Set to work, all of you! We've got a ship to ready if we're to shove off by midafternoon."

The men scrambled to their feet, some cursing as they went. I didn't mind the cursing or the scowls, for as long as they did their duties it made no difference to me. One man in particular, Robert Lynch, immediately went aloft to see about the rigging. He was a young man, mid-twenties; a mop of brown shaggy hair adorned his large head and a long neck extended beneath his chin. He was a scrawny fellow, but strong and a natural leader.

When the Royal Navy defeated me and my crew on board the *Rebecca,* I was saddened to find one of the casualties was the ships boatswain, Isaac Norington. Norington had been a trusted member of my crew for two years and his stern demeanor was respected by every man on the ship. He would be a difficult man to replace, but I truly felt young Robert Lynch would be up for the job.

I strolled over to the rail nearest where the young man was working.

"Good morning, Robert," I said jovially.

He stopped fumbling with the rope in his hands and gazed down upon me.

"Good morning, Captain. Beautiful weather for sailing," he replied with a smile.

"Aye, it is. Robert, I was wondering if I may ask a favor of you."

The smile he'd been wearing vanished and his face turned serious. His brown eyes widened.

"Of course, sir. What do you need?"

"As you know, Isaac Norington was cut down by the redcoats when our ship was taken five days ago," I began.

Robert's serious expression turned somber as he thought of Norington. He nodded in acknowledgement.

"His death puts me in an unfortunate predicament a mere few hours away from setting sail," I said. "It's hard to replace a man like Norington and, well, I just feel you'd be perfect for the job if you're interested."

"Are you asking me to be boatswain, Captain Redd?" the young man asked in disbelief.

"What say you? Are you up for the task?"

Robert opened his mouth to answer, but was cut off suddenly by the shrill voice of "Jolly" Jack Porter, the ship's cook who had apparently been eavesdropping on the conversation from nearby. He was a wise old bloke with lots of stories. When he spoke, the other pirates listened. He only had three fingers on his right hand (the other two were cut off during a raid of a Spanish fort over ten years ago), but he pointed the remaining ragged digits straight up at Robert.

"Robert is a fine choice, Cap'n," he said. "It's for certain he is… and you better accept the offer, laddie, or I'll give you a swift kick in the arse."

Robert smiled, and I couldn't help but chuckle.

"You heard Jolly Jack," I said. "I think the matter is settled."

Robert shook his head and gazed out to sea, way beyond the harbor. I could tell he was still mulling it over. I leaned closer to him in an effort to keep the rest of our conversation more private.

"Robert, I haven't forgotten your reason for turning to piracy six years ago," I said softly.

He whipped his head in my direction, his eyes narrowed and a flicker of fury burned there a moment.

"What are you saying, Captain?"

"I'm saying that the *prize* you seek is within reach now," I replied slyly.

"If what you say is true, then I'd be honored to be your boatswain, sir," he agreed quickly. "I swear upon my life that I will do my duties to the absolute best of my ability."

"I do not doubt you," I replied. "Now, are you ready for your first task?"

Robert stared at me; a somewhat surprised look appeared on his face. He seemed taken off guard with his first order as boatswain coming so soon. He hurriedly climbed down from the rigging and stood tall before me.

"Yes, of course, Captain. What do you need?"

"Go into town and fetch the rest of the crew. There's no need to tell them of your new position just yet. I'll do that honor once we set sail."

Robert's eager mood suddenly became more subdued and his shoulders slumped.

"Is something wrong?" I asked.

"No sir—well, it's just... what if they won't listen to me, Captain?"

"Then we'll bloody leave the worthless scugs behind, Robert," I snapped. "However, I don't expect many of them to give you a lot of resistance. After so narrowly escaping the gallows, they'll probably be eager to pull up anchor. I plan to be at sea just before dusk."

"Aye, sir. I'll be back on board in time," he replied.

I watched Robert jog down the gangplank until he disappeared in the vast crowds hurrying about on the streets. I turned back to the men that remained. They continued to do their duties, and I trusted them to do so in my absence.

I turned away and set off for the gangplank. Andrea began to follow and no sooner had I set foot onto the plank, I noticed a trio of red coats walking up the other end. I took a step back to let them board.

Andrea looked at me uneasily and pulled her wide brimmed hat down over her eyes. I was suddenly very grateful for the change of clothes John had given her the night before. She had wisely taken a moment to change before settling in for the night. The soldiers immediately looked her way and watched her curiously for a moment. Next, they scanned over the rest of my crew. They looked upon the men as if they were nothing more than cockroaches.

"Captain, I'm sure by now you've heard about the incident that occurred last night," one of the soldiers said. I immediately recognized his voice; he was the soldier that conducted the search on John's wagon the night before. His appearance was pretty much as I pictured. His straight blonde hair was brought up into a ponytail upon the back of his head. He had a thinly trimmed mustache and blue eyes that seemed to be set slightly too far apart. He seemed to point his stubby nose and cleft chin upward as he spoke to me. The other two soldiers flanked him on both sides, stone-faced. I guessed that he outranked both of them.

"I'm afraid I haven't heard about any *incident*," I replied coolly. "What the devil happened?"

The two soldiers on either side of him suddenly peered at me with smug expressions. I heard one of them stifle a laugh. Their leader, Blondie, flashed his white teeth at me and shook his head.

"Mr. Reeves, I think I should tell you immediately that I do not appreciate liars. In fact, I despise them. Pirates, such as you, are notorious liars." His eyes narrowed and his blue eyes seemed to grow darker. "*Don't* lie to me, Mr. Reeves. I'm going to ask you again; do you know anything about last night's incident?"

I wasn't very surprised by the soldier's attitude since I'd become acquainted with it during the night. He seemed to be pushing me rather quickly. I probably should have refrained from pushing back, but I just didn't want to.

"Do you have a name, soldier?" I asked.

"Flynn… Augustus Flynn," he answered proudly.

"Right. Mr. Flynn, first of all when you address me, you shall call me Captain Reeves." I watched his eyes widen in disbelief. "Secondly, I answered your question once, and if you accuse me of lying once again I'm going to make you eat those bloody words."

Flynn's face turned so red I feared his bloody eyes would pop out. The other soldier's faces were white in contrast. Clearly, this Mr. Flynn wasn't used to being talked to in this fashion. Flynn reached down and drew his sword. I took a step back and reached for my cutlass and suddenly realized I'd left it in the cabin. Flynn stepped toward me and held the tip of his sword to my chin. I heard Andrea gasp and I caught sight of two of my men watching the scene intensely. They seemed ready and willing to pounce if and when I needed them. I gave them a look that they were familiar with. *Stand down.* I backed up until my legs touched the railing. Flynn moved his face inches from mine.

"The only reason I will not slice your throat down to the neck bone is because Governor Winters gave me explicit instructions to inflict no physical harm," he snarled, moisture spraying from his lips.

"The governor sent you, did he?" I asked.

"*Do not* interrupt me, pirate!"

I held up both hands in surrender. There was nothing I could do with a sword against my throat.

"The governor *did* indeed send me," he continued. "My inquiry about last night's events was merely a preface to my real reason for being here."

"Which is?" I asked sheepishly.

Flynn kept his sword pointed toward my throat, but he seemed to relax a bit. He knew he'd gotten the better of me this time and he seemed to relish it. Then he smiled, and suddenly I began to wonder where all of this was going.

Did Winters have a change of heart? Were we on the verge of being arrested once again?

If that were indeed the case, surely the governor would not have been foolish enough to send only three men to carry out the feat. I dismissed the notion and anxiously waited for Flynn to tell me more.

"We are interested in a certain member of your crew," he said.

I arched an eyebrow.

"Who exactly are *we*?" I asked, bewildered.

Flynn's evil, toothy smile returned and he finally dropped the sword by his side.

"I'll cut to the chase," he replied. "Specifically, his majesty King George is the interested party. It seems a man on your crew was mistakenly released yesterday. The governor has ordered me to retrieve him."

I shook my head, confusion washing over me.

"Retrieve him for what?" I asked.

"He is wanted for a murder that occurred over five years ago."

I immediately knew the name of the man they were looking for, but I forced myself to ask the question anyway.

"What is the man's name?"

"Gordon Littleton," Flynn replied. "He has blonde hair, dresses well, and practices good hygiene. In other words, he isn't your typical pirate."

Flynn's two sidekicks laughed at their leader's jibe. I looked over Flynn's shoulder and saw Jolly Jack Porter watching and listening to our exchange. I gave him a reassuring smile and then turned my attention back to Flynn.

"I'm afraid I haven't seen Mr. Littleton since last night," I said with conviction.

Flynn's relaxed demeanor seemed to evaporate all at once. He began to lightly slap the blade of his sword against his leg. The gesture made me nervous.

"You're lying once again, pirate," he growled with extra emphasis on the word *pirate*.

"No, I am not," I countered. "I've been looking for him all morning. He's my navigator, and I must confess I've come to depend on him a little too much. It shames me to say I've become a bit rusty when it comes to charts and such." I crossed my arms and sighed. "As a matter of fact, it'll probably be better for you to find him at this point than me," I said coldly.

Flynn stared at me with genuine confusion.

"For Gordon's sake, I mean," I tried to clarify. I glanced at Jolly Jack again. "We haven't had a good keel-hauling in quite a while, have we, Jack?"

"Harr! That be true, Cap'n," he replied, facing Flynn. "We don't treat deserters very kindly on Cap'n Redd's vessel, mate."

Flynn studied Jolly Jack a long moment and then looked back at me.

"Captain, you will let me know at once if you come into contact with Mr. Littleton," he said. I took the fact that he referred to me as *captain* as a sign that he bought the story.

"I'll do just that, Mr. Flynn."

He turned away to leave and then suddenly spun back around on his heel. He held the sword up to my face again.

"You'd better not be lying about this or I'll cut your heart out," he snapped.

I gently took my hat off my head and held it to my chest.

"May I sink and perish in me own blood if I'm lying," I replied.

Flynn smiled, apparently satisfied with my oath. He placed the sword back in its sheath and began to retreat back toward the gangplank, his two sidekicks in tow.

I breathed a heavy sigh of utter relief. I looked over at Andrea, whom I'd forgotten was nearby, and the poor lass was white as a ghost. Although pale, there was obvious relief in her face as well.

Suddenly the door of the captain's cabin burst open and Gordon clambered out onto the deck.

"Where's my bloody breakfast?" he barked, almost incoherently.

My heart dropped and I quickly motioned for Gordon to return to the cabin. It was obvious he was still feeling the effects from the head injury he'd sustained because he immediately fell toward the railing I was leaned against. I grabbed him to try and keep the man from falling overboard and he in turn proceeded to vomit profusely. I glanced back toward the gangplank, fearful that Augustus Flynn would be returning.

I looked on in horror as my worst fears became reality.

"Who is that man?" Flynn asked, pointing and marching aggressively back on deck.

"Him?" I asked, pointing at the back of Gordon's head. "He's no one." It was the only pathetic retort I could muster.

Flynn strode past me and grabbed Gordon by the hair on the back of his head. When he saw his face, his cold eyes narrowed again and he scowled at me. The look in his eyes told me what was coming, and I immediately darted away and jumped over a nearby banister where Jolly Jack was standing.

Flynn said nothing. He reached to his side and unsheathed his sword again. Jolly Jack pulled his own cutlass from its scabbard and tossed it to me. Flynn began marching toward me and I prepared for a duel to the death.

"Augustus, you mustn't engage him!"

To my surprise, the voice I heard originated from one of his sidekicks whom, up to this point, had said and done nothing.

Flynn ignored him and kept marching my way. I backed up as he approached, desperately hoping the accompanying soldiers would intervene.

"Augustus," the other man said. "Do not forget what your uncle said! You must not harm him!"

Uncle? I thought. *Governor Winters is this scoundrel's uncle?*

This time, the plea seemed to reach him. Flynn stopped suddenly, but he shook violently. There was an incredible rage building inside him, and it seemed as if he'd explode like a volcano if it wasn't released.

The other two soldiers grabbed Gordon and began leading him down the gangplank.

"What sort of scum are you?" I heard one of them say. "Murdering your own wife? What a coward you are!"

Flynn reluctantly returned his sword to its sheath, his glaring eyes still locked onto me.

"We will conclude this at another time, pirate," he snarled.

I watched helplessly as the three soldiers escorted Gordon away. Whether it was shame or maybe he was simply unable, Gordon never looked back at me and never put forth any resistance. He said not one word as they led him away. When they were finally out of sight I slammed my fist onto a nearby banister.

"There was nothing you could do," Andrea said softly.

"I should've cut down that wretched vermin," I roared back. "I will not leave this port without Gordon... I won't!" I squeezed the railing tightly and did my best to turn the timber into sawdust.

Andrea strolled toward me and placed her soft hand on top of mine. Her touch seemed to instantly calm me.

"You cannot save him," she pleaded. "He will be heavily guarded."

I glared at her. "So were you. It didn't stop us from rescuing you, now did it?"

She frowned and momentarily looked away.

"They will not allow a repeat of what occurred last night," she continued. "Surely you know that!"

I did know it. What she said was absolute truth. There would be no way for me to rescue Gordon, yet I had to try! I believed he would do the same for me.

Langley suddenly appeared on deck, and he approached me sober and wild-eyed.

"Jolly Jack just told me what happened," he said anxiously. "What are we going to do, Cap'n?"

"We're going to get Gordon back," I replied much to his delight.

"Aye, Cap'n," he said, holding his cutlass into the air. "My blade is sharp enough to cut through the entire Royal Navy if need be."

"No! This is madness!" Andrea shouted.

Langley lowered his weapon, and the two of us stared at her.

"If you try to help Mr. Littleton escape, you may as well go ahead and tie your noose right here and now," she said. "We must stick to our plan and sail this afternoon. We can make it to New Providence in less than a week downwind."

Once again, I considered what Andrea was saying and I knew that she was right. As my heart and mind played tug-of-war on what to do, I suddenly thought of one more possible avenue I could take to try and get Gordon back. It was a long shot, but it was the only idea I had left.

"Langley, I'm leaving you in charge. I've sent Robert into town to round up the crew, but while he is away I need every man on this ship working double time to make certain we set sail before dusk."

I peered up at the sloop's mainmast; I had to cup my hand over my eyes to shield the sun.

"I know little of this ship so I'm counting on you to explore every nook and cranny she's got." I paused a moment and stifled a laugh as another thought popped into my head. "I don't even know the name of this bloody vessel."

"Her name's *Henrietta*," Jolly Jack explained. "She's a fine sloop, Cap'n. I shared drinks with a few red coats in the Parrot's Landing last night," he said. "I inquired about the ship and those blokes were so drunk they happily answered all of my questions. She's one of the fastest in their fleet. I'm afraid she's only got six guns on each side, though," he finished, frowning.

"We'll make sure to get the most out of all twelve of them," I replied. "Just make sure she's ready to set sail when I return."

"Aye, Cap'n," Langley and Jack said in unison.

I turned away and began to exit the ship. Andrea caught my arm as I went by.

"And what about me?" she asked.

"What about you?"

"May I come along?"

I shook my head. "You know you can't be seen strolling around town. Stay here and help these men ready the ship."

"Where are you going?"

"To pay the governor one more visit," I replied through clenched teeth.

Chapter 6

It was unfortunate that I didn't have a horse because the walk to the King's House, where the governor resided, was a long one. I traveled by foot through the bustling city streets until I reached the outskirts of the city. There was a long, dusty road that led to the top of a hill on which the King's House sat in all its majestic glory.

Palm trees littered the grounds surrounding the structure, and there were numerous floral gardens behind and to the right of the building as well. The structure itself was a beautiful three-story mansion painted white with six enormous columns that stood tall and intimidating across the front wall.

I began the trek up the driveway and as I approached the iron gate two guards spotted me and began to ready their weapons.

"Beautiful day, isn't it?" I asked them, trying to break the ice.

"What is your business here, sir?" one of them asked me.

I pulled my tricorn from my head and held it in both hands in an attempt to look as less threatening as possible.

"I need to speak with the governor at once," I said. "It's most urgent."

The guards seemed to relax a bit but kept their voices firm.

"No one is allowed to just walk up to the gate and ask for the governor, sir." The guard spoke to me as if he were speaking to a child. "Even if you *were* allowed to visit with the governor, I'm afraid he isn't even here."

The other soldier sighed deeply and darted his green eyes at his counterpart in annoyance.

"Do not discuss the governor's affairs with this man," he spat. "We don't know him from Adam's housecat."

The other soldier's eyes seemed to widen as he realized his mistake. He nodded in agreement.

"Be gone, sir," he said. "If you want to speak to the governor I suggest you do it through one of his aides at the courthouse. You may even try the town hall."

I rang the hat in my hands as I fought hard to keep my composure.

"Dear sirs, you both seem like a couple of fine soldiers and I realize you're just doing your jobs, but—"

"You're not going to be speaking with the governor today, laddie," the gruff, green-eyed soldier interrupted. "Now we told you how to go about reaching him so go on and be on your way now." He gestured his free hand to *shoo* me away.

I felt my blood pressure begin to rise. I smiled widely in an effort to hide my displeasure.

"Gentlemen, I think I may have failed to mention that I am a personal friend of the governor," I said calmly.

The demeanor of both men seemed to change instantly when I said that, and I could tell I'd just gotten their interest. They both eyed me a long moment before Green Eyes spoke again.

"So, what's your name, lad?" he asked.

"If I tell you, will you let me see him?"

The soldier sighed again.

"We already told you, boy, the governor is not here."

"Then where is he?" I demanded a little too forcefully.

Green Eyes seemed taken aback with my tone. He stepped forward and I instinctively stepped backwards. He reached a large, gloved hand toward me, but then stopped suddenly. I noticed him gazing over my shoulder and down the road. He jerked his hand back and returned to his post promptly as if nothing had happened. I turned to see what had rattled him and spotted a carriage rumbling along in our direction.

"Looks like you bloody well got your wish," the soldier barked. "It seems the governor is returning home early."

I gave him a smug expression and then crossed my arms as the carriage came to a stop. The soldiers opened the gate for the carriage to pass through, but as it pulled alongside me, its driver pulled the reigns, stopping it suddenly. The door swung open and Governor Winters popped his head out into the midday sun. He had a look of surprise upon his face.

"What the devil are *you* doing here?" he snapped.

"I'm afraid you know exactly why I'm here," I answered back. "Your nephew paid me a visit this morning and left with an important member of my crew."

Governor Winter's scowled at me but motioned for me to come inside the carriage. He then ordered his driver to give us a moment to chat. It was a pleasant day, but the inside of the carriage seemed stuffy. The governor fanned himself to keep cool. I was seated across from him and suddenly found myself doing the same thing with my hat.

"I'm beginning to regret my decision to free you, Captain Reeves," he said.

"I want Gordon back at once," I snapped.

He leaned forward and poked a finger toward me. "Is this how you repay my kindness? By showing up at my home unannounced and making demands?"

"Governor, you need me to do a job for you. I *need* Gordon desperately to perform this job."

"The man is wanted for murder!" he replied. "There are wanted posters all over this city with his bloody face on them. The king demands that he be returned to London at once. What would you have me do? Disobey a direct order from the king?"

"Haven't you, in essence, already done so by releasing us yesterday?" I asked.

The words I'd just spoken seem to strike him like a slap in the face. His beady eyes narrowed into nasty slits and I saw his jaw clench.

"I'm doing what I think is necessary to save countless lives from a crazed pirate!" he erupted. "The seas will not be safe until Captain Trimble is disposed of. *That* is why I did what I did. If you recall, *you* were the only pirate I originally wanted to release, but I allowed you to talk me into handing over the rest of your worthless crew! Gordon Littleton is not my concern and you will find a way to accomplish your goals without his help. If you're unable to do so, I will be happy to lock the lot of you back into the cold dark cell from whence you came. Now get out of my sight!"

He threw the door open and motioned for me to get out. Reluctantly, I stepped out. He began to pull the door shut but I grabbed it suddenly.

"What will happen to him?" I asked softly without looking at him.

"Tomorrow morning Captain Edward Sutton will set sail with Mr. Littleton locked away in the brig of *Neptune's Castle*. Two months from now they should arrive in London where Mr. Littleton will be tried and hanged for his crimes of piracy and murder. Does that answer your question? Good day, sir." He jerked the door from my hand and slammed it loudly.

I clenched my fists as the carriage continued toward the mansion. Once through the gate, the two soldiers quickly shut it and watched me cautiously as if they were expecting me to hurry after the governor once more.

I slowly turned away from them and began my trek back to the sloop *Henrietta*. I thought of everything the governor had said, and suddenly my dejection began to lift as a daring plan began to form in my head. I smiled and my slow walk evolved into a run.

By the time I returned to the ship, Robert Lynch had returned with every missing member of the crew. Many of the men were hung over and sickly, but it did not concern me. I knew that the sea was the best medicine for these sorts of men and it would not be long before we pulled up anchor.

Andrea and Langley approached as soon as I boarded and they had two very different reactions after I told them what had happened with the governor. Langley was furious and still adamant that we storm the prison and free Gordon before leaving the city. Andrea, to my dismay, seemed almost relieved that the governor refused my pleas. I can only assume that she believed this would force me to give up hope of ever rescuing Gordon. She would soon find that she had a lot to learn about me.

I was about to reveal my plan when I noticed no fewer than twenty African men huddled near the poop deck. I turned to Robert for an explanation.

"They were here when I got back," he answered defensively.

"Several redcoats brought them aboard about an hour ago," Andrea explained. "They said the governor sent them to you as compensation."

"Compensation?" I asked in awe. "For Gordon?"

"That is what I assumed as well," she replied.

I cursed silently to myself and wished that I had known of the governor's plan to "compensate" me for the loss of Gordon before

I'd visited him. I'd have gladly told him to keep his slaves because they would be of little use to me.

I eyed the poor-spirited men and they stared back at me with confusion. There was a strong urge to send them off the ship and on their merry way. But where would they go? The life that they'd been living couldn't have been a very pleasant one, and it was one they probably didn't want to return to. A life at sea would probably be far better than the one they were currently living, and I had the power to offer them that.

"Is there one among you that speaks English?" I asked hopefully.

Several of them stepped forward.

"Is there one among you that would be allowed to speak for your group alone with me in private quarters?"

One of the slaves stepped forward and pointed to his chest as if to indicate that he was the willing party to speak for the group. I estimated his age to be late thirties. The first thing I noticed about him was his hands. They were quite large and seemed closer to the size of a bear's paw than a man's hand. He was a large, tall man, and except for Hale Woodrow, he was easily larger than any other man on my crew. The man's head was bald and smooth as a baby's bottom. The lower portion of his face was covered in at least a day's worth of stubble. He wore a dirty white linen shirt and calico pants. As was with all of his counterparts, there were no shoes on his feet.

I led him into the captain's cabin and Andrea started to follow us in as well. I leaned over so only she could hear me.

"I'd rather speak with him alone, my dear," I said softly.

She gave me a disappointed look that briefly turned to anger, but finally walked away to help the rest of the crew without another word. I watched her a moment and a bad feeling struck me. I needed her help in finding her father, but I still did not know if I could trust her. She seemed cold and uncaring regarding the situation with Gordon, and it seemed that the more I got to know her, the more abrasive her personality was becoming. I assumed, and hoped, this was due to the fact that she was Captain Trimble's own blood. Surely some of his horrible traits passed on to his daughter. However, that in itself was troubling for me as well.

I sat down on one side of the heavy oak table and the slave sat on the other. I reached across the table to shake his hand. The big man took it and his handshake was firm yet gentle.

"My name is Captain Redd Reeves," I began. "There is no easy way to say this, so I'll just come out with it. I'm a known pirate and so are the other members of my crew. The governor sent you and your lot to me in hopes that you would accompany me on a perilous mission. It seems he's placing you in my custody against your will."

I paused a moment to see if I noticed any indication that the man was angry or uncomfortable. There was none of that in his eyes. He stared at me with wide-eyed, genuine interest of what I had to say.

"However," I continued. "We are pirates and rogues, and the life we live is far different from the world you're accustomed to in Port Royal. We do not believe a man can take possession of another man and force him to do his bidding. I want men that are willing and able to fight at my side. A pirate's life is not always an easy one and all men are free to go if they please. The way I see it, the governor placed you in my custody and thus, you all have become pirates. If it pleases you to walk off this ship, you will get no resistance from me and my crew."

The large man smiled a wide grin filled with the whitest and straightest teeth I'd ever seen. It was still hot in the cabin, and both of us were sweating profusely. I could not be sure, but there appeared to be a tear streaming down the right side of his face.

"That is very good of you, Captain," he said in surprisingly clean English. "I will ask the other men what they think about it." He paused and adjusted in his chair. "If it's okay with you, Captain, I would be just fine staying on the ship," he said meekly.

I leaned back and crossed my arms.

"I haven't gotten your name yet, sir."

"Jobah, Captain, my name is Jobah," he replied. "Most people just call me Joe."

"Well, what do *you* want to be called?"

"Joe is just fine with me, sir."

"Okay, Joe it is then. Joe, do you have any experience at sea?"

Joe lowered his head and closed his eyes as if in thought. "No sir, I remember being on a boat when I was a boy, but that's about it."

I cringed when I realized he was referring to his time on a slave boat. It had to be a troubling memory for him as I'd heard about the harsh conditions slaves were put through on those long voyages from Africa to the new world.

"Joe, as I said in the beginning, we are about to embark on a perilous mission. A pirate's life is not an easy one and you will have much to learn. I will not lie to you; there is a strong possibility of death almost every day." I paused a moment to let the weight of the words sink in. "Are you sure this is the life you would choose for yourself?"

Joe sat quietly and thought hard about what I'd said. He finally looked me in the eyes and gave me an answer I'd never forget.

"If the pirate life is a free one, then it is the one for me," he said.

I grinned and shook his hand again.

"Welcome to the crew, Joe."

I followed him as he exited the cabin and watched him gather the other slaves to tell them of the opportunity I'd laid before them. After much deliberation, half of the men made their way to the gangplank and returned to the city of Port Royal. The others approached and made their allegiance known to me.

I called upon Robert Lynch to take the remaining nine men below deck and gain each one's signature upon the articles for pirate service. Most of the men were unable to write, but with great patience Robert and Joe managed to get each man to scrawl out a single letter or symbol to solidify their allegiance.

While they were below deck, I peered out at the numerous ships in the harbor in search of one in particular.

"The governor said that Gordon would be taken in the morning on a ship called *Neptune's Castle*," I murmured to Langley.

Andrea was standing nearby, and at mention of the ship, her face lit up and she grabbed my arm.

"I know of that ship!" she said.

Langley and I looked at her inquisitively and awaited an explanation.

"That is the ship that picked me up from the island my father marooned me on," she explained. "It's a massive English galleon; it's truly a beautiful ship."

"It's a galleon?" I asked, disheartened by the news.

"Yes, she bear's no less than forty guns and a crew of at least a hundred fifty," she replied.

"Do you see the ship in this harbor," I asked, waving an outstretched hand in the direction of the array of various ships that blanketed the calm waters of the day.

She pulled the brim of her hat down to shield the piercing sunlight from her eyes and squinted as she peered in the direction where many of the Royal Navy's ships were anchored.

"Yes, I think that one is it," she said, pointing.

"I need to bring 'er near, Langley," I said, squinting against the glint of the sun sparkled waters.

Langley disappeared a moment and promptly returned with a brass telescope. I took aim for the vessel and looked her over the best I could.

"She is a fine vessel," I said, tossing the scope back to Langley. "Though I was hoping for a smaller ship indeed."

Andrea looked at me at first with confusion, but then her expression turned to shock as she realized what I'd been plotting.

"You can't be serious!" she snapped.

I glanced at her and said nothing.

"Look at the ship you're standing on, Captain," she pleaded, her blonde hair blowing wildly in a sudden, misty breeze. "This ship is only a sloop and is incapable of defeating a ship the caliber of *Neptune's Castle.* You must rethink this. One man is not worth the countless deaths your crew will suffer!"

I leaned toward the ship's rail and grabbed it tightly. I looked around and noticed many of the crew watching and listening to our exchange. I grabbed Andrea by the arm and rather forcefully led her away and into my cabin so we could continue the conversation in private. I shoved her toward a chair and she reluctantly sat down; I could tell she could see the obvious anger in my expression.

"I'm a pirate captain, Andrea—"

"And a rather stupid one, it would seem," she interrupted. "We should keep our current heading of New Providence. Every day you wait, my father will grow more comfortable with the signet ring and his boldness will grow as well. It's only a matter of time before he will have both the English and Spanish Navies at their knees."

"I will not let that happen!"

"Then do as I say and forget this folly with Mr. Littleton!"

I felt my face redden with rage, and it was fortunate for Andrea that she was a woman, as I would have struck her had she been a man.

"Andrea, you asked me to look at the ship I'm standing on, did you not?"

"Yes," she replied.

"Then I would ask you to do the same."

"What is the point of this ridiculous exercise?"

"You said yourself that this ship is incapable of bringing down *Neptune's Castle*. So I ask you now if you feel that it *is* capable of bringing down your father's flagship the *Sea Witch*."

"Well of course not," she replied. "I planned to seek out a proper ship in New Providence."

"I had the same ideas," I admitted. "However, I now have a plan that would allow us to kill two birds with one stone."

She eyed me suspiciously and it was obvious she knew exactly what I was planning.

"Are you saying you plan on rescuing Gordon and taking *Neptune's Castle*?"

I nodded.

She seemed to relax in the chair and I could tell her interest had peaked.

"I'm listening," she said.

I pulled up a chair and sat in it backwards, facing her. I leaned against the back and began to reveal my scheme.

"This ship is obviously a sloop, and what are sloops known for?" I asked.

"Speed, of course," she replied.

"Yes, that's right," I agreed. "We will set sail tonight as planned, but instead of heading to New Providence we will set a course for Tortuga."

"Tortuga?" she asked with disgust in her tone.

"I have a friend in Tortuga that owes me a favor. He has a large enough vessel with enough men and cannons to take *Neptune's Castle*. I'll bet we can make enough speed with this sloop to make it there in under a day's time. The head start is all we need to put a plan in place and intercept *Neptune's Castle* on its way back to England."

"Wait a minute," Andrea interrupted. "I thought this plan would involve you taking *Neptune's Castle* for your own. She won't be of any use to you if you blow holes in her hull."

"Of course she wouldn't," I agreed. "The main goal is to get Gordon back. If I have to blow the ship apart to get him, then I will." As her face began to redden, it was quite obvious that those were not the words she wanted to hear. "However," I continued, "it's in our best interest to try and get Gordon back without damaging the ship. Ricardo is an intelligent man and is notorious for using trickery to overtake another ship. I'm sure between the two of us we'll be able to come up with a good plan."

"I assume that Ricardo is the friend you speak of in Tortuga," she replied.

"Aye, he's been an ally of mine for a long time. Our crews have raided at least a dozen treasure galleons across the Caribbean side by side. Five days ago, when the Royal Navy captured me and my men, Ricardo and his crew were briefly in the fight but managed to escape. It seems that the Royal Navy wasn't nearly as interested in capturing Ricardo as they were me. While the redcoats were busy slaughtering my crew, Ricardo slipped away."

"So this is where the favor you speak of comes into the picture," Andrea said. "How do you even know he is in Tortuga?"

"That was our last heading before the battle with the Royal Navy," I explained. "There is a woman in Tortuga that Ricardo has grown quite fond of and he's taken up permanent residence there. Last we spoke, he was looking forward to seeing her again and once he arrives there he's not going to set sail again right way. Not after seeing me captured, anyway. He'll hide out for at least a week, maybe two."

Andrea pursed her lips and glanced out to sea as she considered my plan.

"Alright," she said finally. "Tortuga is only slightly off course from New Providence. Are you sure we can trust this man?"

"Ricardo?" I asked, trying to sound offended that she'd even question me. "He is the epitome of a cutthroat and has a far darker side than I."

"Yes, that's exactly why I'd like to know if we can trust him," she quipped.

"I think so," I answered. "But, he *did* slip away while my crew was being slaughtered by the red coats."

She crossed her arms and cocked her head sideways, smiling.

"Exactly!" she said. "You *can't* trust him."

I shrugged my shoulders.

"Okay, I admit that it's a tiny gamble."

"*Tiny?*" she squealed in an exaggerated tone of disbelief.

"Well, it's a more thought-out plan than anything you've offered up so far," I countered.

She remained still, arms crossed. She didn't bother arguing my point, most likely because she knew my mind was already made up. An hour later, we were sailing on a northeasterly course for Tortuga.

Chapter 7

The voyage to Tortuga was swift and uneventful. *Henrietta* glided into the island's port shortly after noon with a very drunk Oliver Langley at the helm. As soon as we'd lost sight of Jamaica, I made the announcement of Robert's promotion as boatswain. As expected, the crew was supportive of my choice but did not shy away from taking a few japes at the well-liked lad as well. They would test him, I knew, but I believed he would rise to be the leader I envisioned him to be.

The next order of business was to fill the men in on the circumstances surrounding their release. This was a topic I knew I'd have to handle delicately, and although I'd have been fine with just avoiding it altogether, I owed them and promised them an explanation. I cut to the chase and quickly disclosed the deal I'd made with the governor. The men's expressions turned from eager anticipation to shock and dread as soon as the part about pursuing Captain Trimble was revealed.

Once again, I decided to keep the details regarding King Solomon's signet ring to myself just as I had done with Langley and Gordon. Again, I felt guilt, but I did my best to squash those feelings by telling myself there was no need to get the men any more horrified that they already were. Trimble was frightening enough without a magical ring in the mix. Andrea glared at me suspiciously as she realized that I was keeping the tale of the ring and King Solomon from the crew. For a moment, I feared that she would expose my deception, but fortunately she held her tongue.

Joe and his nine counterparts took to the sea better than I'd anticipated. Only two of the former slaves became ill. I wouldn't have blamed them for requesting to be released upon our arrival in Tortuga, but neither man did anything of the sort. They both took to their chores as if they felt they had to catch up on what they'd fallen behind on during the voyage due to sickness. The rest of the crew seemed to embrace the former slaves much faster than I would have guessed. Perhaps it was because they knew it was in their best interest to get their new shipmates accustomed to life on a pirate ship as soon as possible. The men seemed to catch onto the fundamentals of sailing relatively quickly. My crew was a rough-looking lot of scoundrels, but I would never question their intelligence.

Once we dropped anchor, Langley immediately stumbled below deck and collapsed onto the first hammock in his path. Andrea eyed the somewhat comical spectacle with fascination.

"I've been around men who drank worse than the largest fish in the sea," she said. "But I've never seen a man drink as much as Langley in such a short period of time and live to tell the tale."

"If that impresses you, wait and see how quickly he sleeps it off," I replied. "He'll be sober as a baby in a few hours' time."

She shook her head. "I'll have to see that one for myself before I believe it, Captain."

Andrea then gave a quick glance both directions and drew near to me. "I couldn't help but notice you left out a few details regarding my father and a certain piece of jewelry he possesses," she whispered.

I let out a sigh that could've been taken as an expression of shame.

"I just don't feel it's anything they need to be burdened with right now," I explained. "I'll tell them the whole truth when the time is right."

Andrea said nothing in response; she just turned her gaze toward the docks as some of the crew began to file down the gangplank. Her silence made me curious.

"Do you disagree with my decision?" I asked.

She quickly turned back toward me, doe-eyed.

"Oh no, of course not," she replied. "It's actually a smart move in my opinion."

"Really?" I said, somewhat surprised. "Do you mind explaining?"

"My father is not a man one would chase after for the fun of it," she said. "He's a monster, a blood-thirsty shark, and his men are just like him. It's going to be hard enough for your men to defeat the crew of the *Sea Witch* without having to worry about magic and sea monsters too."

I crossed my arms and leaned my back against the railing next to her.

"Tell me about your father," I said.

Andrea smiled and took a step away from me.

"What would you like to know?" she asked, turning back to face me.

"What makes men fear him so much—I mean before he got the ring. After all, he is just a man, same as me," I replied.

She stared at me for a moment and her eyes suddenly turned cold and deadly serious.

"My father is no ordinary man," she said bluntly.

"What do you mean?"

"My father does not feel pain as you and I do."

I snickered and stood upright, off the railing.

"I bloody doubt that," I argued. "All men feel pain."

"Yes, of course he feels *some* pain, but it's not the same as you and I," she sneered. "Have you ever seen my father?"

"No, if I had one of us would probably be dead today," I replied.

"True. If you had seen my father you'd know that the entire left side of his body is covered in hideous scars."

"I've heard he wears a patch over his left eye," I said.

"Yes, that is because when he was much younger—before he ever became a captain—a terrible event occurred that molded him into the monster you've heard stories about. He was a young deck hand and already seasoned in the trade of piracy. The ship he was on was attacked by another pirate ship and a violent battle occurred in which almost all of his crew was killed. Their ship was destroyed and burned. He'd been shot and left for dead on board the burning ship. He told me that when he lost consciousness his body was on fire and he fully expected to wake up in hell. To his surprise, this did not happen and he instead awoke several days later with almost his entire body wrapped in bandages. He told me that he'd never endured pain like what he experienced the many weeks and months after he'd awakened. As time passed, his body began to heal, and terrible scars were left on half of his body. He also lost the sight in his left eye and all feeling and sensation escaped that side of his body as well. To this day he still feels nothing on the entire left side of his body. You can bury the steel of your cutlass down to the bone in his left shoulder and he will not flinch."

I stood there in awe as I listened to Andrea's story, and I could feel the blood flood away from my face as I was struck by an epiphany. Andrea could tell by the look in my eyes that she'd struck a chord.

"Captain, what's wrong?" she asked softly.

I shook my head and paced past her as I replayed the events in my head. She chased after me and I stopped suddenly to face her.

"That ship that attacked the vessel your father was on…"

"Yes?"

"Do you know the name of it?"

I closed my eyes and tensed as I anticipated her response.

"No," she replied. "I'm sorry, but I do not know the name of the ship."

I released a sigh of relief and my whole body seemed to relax.

"I'm sorry," she said, apparently misinterpreting my body language as an indication of disappointment.

"No, no—you don't understand," I said. "It's nothing to apologize for."

She suddenly perked up and it seemed she'd suddenly experienced an epiphany of her own.

"I remember hearing the name of the ship's captain if that will help," she offered a tad too cheerfully.

The tension suddenly returned and I felt a headache coming on.

"What was his name?" I asked reluctantly.

"Captain Douglas Bloodbane," she replied.

I suddenly felt weak in the knees, but I kept my composure. I wasn't about to let Andrea see me rattled.

"Have you heard of him?" she asked.

I laughed nervously.

"Oh yes, I bloody well knew him," I said. "I sailed under the scurvy bastard."

Andrea's eyes widened as she began to process what I'd said. She grabbed me by both shoulders as if she were about to shake me.

"Well I'll be blown," she said in awe. "You were on the ship that attacked my father, weren't you?"

"I was just a cabin boy and had been pretty much forced into piracy just a few months before it happened," I began, solemnly. "The name of the ship was *Dawn Breaker*. She was a magnificent ship and, at the time, the largest vessel I'd ever seen.

"I remember scrubbing the floors below deck when I suddenly heard the thunder of a cannon off in the distance. The next thing I knew, I was on my back—my ears ringing—and covered in splinters. There was a gaping hole in the starboard side of the hull only a few feet from where I'd been scrubbing."

"So Bloodbane was attacked first?" Andrea asked.

"It certainly seemed that way," I answered. "All I know is that Bloodbane's voice boomed orders from the deck above me and men began scurrying into their battle stations to prepare for a fight to the death. I was told to stay out of the way and only assist when asked. I knelt next to the ragged hole in the side of our ship and got my first glimpse at our attacker. It was an impressive brigantine with at least ten guns on each side. She had large, red square-rigged sales on the foremast and white triangular sails on the mainmast. The ship looked relatively new with its freshly painted hull, and I can only assume her crew was as young and fresh as she was."

"What do you mean?" Andrea asked.

"I just mean that the crew of that ship fought as if they had no clue as to what they were doing. They made many mistakes, and Captain Bloodbane took advantage of them all. *Dawn Breaker* was a slightly larger ship—a galleon—and boasted fifteen guns on each side. Bloodbane veered his ship sharply to eliminate the opportunity for our attacker to get a broadside shot at us again. *Dawn Breaker* had a heading straight for the port side of the other ship. If the enemy wanted to take a shot at us now, they'd have to hit us in the bow, a much smaller target. Captain Bloodbane also had the wind to his advantage, and before the other ship knew it, we were in position to unload all fifteen of *Dawn Breaker*'s starboard cannons into the port side of the other ship."

"Surely the other ship had time to return fire," Andrea assumed.

"Aye, they did," I confirmed. "But as I said, this crew seemed young and green. They're timing was off. We struck first, and most of their gunners must have been killed or injured pretty severely because I only remember three of their cannon's returning fire. To make matters worse, Bloodbane had his men pelt the deck of their ship with grenadoes filled with bits of metal and glass at the same time the cannons fired. Many of the men on deck were swept off their feet as the explosions sent shrapnel tearing through flesh and bone.

"By the time *Dawn Breaker* sailed around for a broadside attack on our enemy's starboard side, its crew was so flustered and bloody, they were unable to fire a single cannon. Their ship was turned to kindling by another barrage of cannon fire."

"What about my father?" Andrea said abruptly. "Where was he in all of this?"

I shook my head.

"I truly don't know, Andrea," I replied. "I remained on the *Dawn Breaker* with a small group of men while the captain and the majority of the crew boarded their wounded adversary. I heard the typical sounds associated with fighting, and the screams of death and agony soon followed. Bloodbane ordered the ship to be set fire and any survivors were left on the ship to burn. Even if I'd have caught a glimpse of Trimble, I wouldn't have known the man from Adam's housecat."

Andrea crossed her arms and let out a sigh.

"Thank you for telling me that," she said.

"There's no need to thank me," I replied.

She shook her head and walked over to me, placing a delicate hand on my shoulder.

"Yes, there is," she said. "There is so little I know about my father. His entire life is a giant puzzle to me. What you just told me was a giant missing piece."

She suddenly seemed teary, and the rollercoaster of emotions concerning her father was beginning to worry me.

"Andrea, there is something I feel that we need to discuss," I said.

She cocked her head in anticipation.

"If everything you've told me is true, we will soon be in New Providence so that you may visit your uncle and get something for me to use as leverage against your father."

Her eyes narrowed.

"Yes, of course," she replied. "I'm not lying to you."

"Okay, well, once you acquire this leverage for me, what happens then?"

She frowned and shook her head.

"I don't understand."

"Sure you do," I replied. "I want to know what happens when you get me what I need to go after your father. You were awfully cooperative in coming up with a plan to find him."

"What are you saying?" she snapped. "Are you trying to insinuate that I would betray you for my father?"

I stared at her.

"Well, you know what they say, love... blood is thicker than water," I answered.

She jabbed a finger into my chest with enough force to inflict a sting of pain.

"My father *marooned* me!" she yelled, tears beginning to flow in earnest. "He marooned his only daughter and left me to die! I love him because he is my father, but do you *really* think I can just overlook the monster that he is? I've seen him do things to other men that would give your nightmares, Redd."

I suddenly felt a pang of shame and guilt for what I'd said.

"Andrea, I—I did not mean to upset you," I stammered. "I just can't imagine a young lass such as yourself basically handing your father a death sentence. It's not something you should have to endure. If you're not up to the task—"

"I'm up to the task," she interrupted, wiping the moisture from her eyes. "My father must receive the death he deserves, and I'll bloody hand it to him myself if need be."

She turned and marched away from me, disappearing into the cabin. I stood there for a moment, dumbfounded and unsure what to make of what had just occurred. Andrea possessed a definite hatred for her father, but I'd seen glimpses of affection for him as well. I supposed it must have been an incredibly difficult and confusing situation for the poor girl, yet... something just didn't seem quite right. I shook the thoughts from my head and turned my attention to the next task at hand. I had to find my old friend Ricardo La Salle, and I knew just where to find him.

The cooking establishment was known simply as Jane's Kitchen. It was a stone-faced, two-story structure with a wooden porch jutting out from the front of the building on the upper level. The interior revealed large oak beams that served as the building's skeleton. There were six tables, all roughly twenty feet long, arranged side by side. Wooden benches flanked the tables and, at present, were covered with the rogues and cutthroats I'd grown accustomed to finding inside this particular establishment.

The men were having a jolly good time. All of them seemed to be more interested in gambling instead of eating; every man present took his turn with dice or cards at some time or another. The jingling sound of coin exchange rang rhythmically with the sound of a guitar strumming off the fingers of a musician in a darkened corner.

I gazed across the motley lot of pirates until I caught sight of Ricardo. He rested in his usual chair, which resembled a throne, at the head of the table nearest the center of the room.

There was a beautiful woman seated upon his lap. Long locks of hair the color of midnight cascaded down her back. She threw her head back in laughter, apparently in response to something Ricardo had said, and it was at that moment the feelings I had for her crept back into the forefront of my mind.

I'd been secretly in love with Jane Mitchell since the first moment I laid eyes upon her. It just so happened that Ricardo and I met the lovely woman at exactly the same time. Ricardo always had a way with women, and that particular day it proved most unfortunate for me. There was no one to blame but myself. It was I that pretended to look upon Jane as if she were an average woman of which I had no particular interest. It was I that encouraged, and all but pushed, Ricardo into approaching her. Knowing these things still did not make it any easier to see the two of them together now.

However difficult it was for me, I always put up an impressive display of indifference in regards to their relationship. This particular time would be no different. Ricardo suddenly noticed my presence and his expression was a mixture of surprise and relief. I suppose this was understandable, as the last time he saw me was during a hopeless situation. He'd barely escaped himself and the truth was that he probably wouldn't have, had it not been for the Royal Navy's relentless pursuit of me. I did not expect Ricardo to express guilt or remorse for leaving me to save his own skin, for it's quite possible that I would have committed the same act. However, what I *did* expect was an expression of unspoken gratitude by way of his willingness to assist me in what I was about to ask of him.

Ricardo made no attempt to call out to me over the noisy pool of pirates that surrounded him. Instead, he raised his arm and waved it back in forth so I'd see him. I locked eyes with him and smiled as I calmly strolled his direction. When I reached him, he gave Jane a soft pat on the leg and when she rose, she immediately awarded me a warm embrace.

"Redd!" she exclaimed. "It's so good to see you again! I have worried about you so much."

She grabbed both my hands and took a step back to look me over. I took a moment to do the same to her. She wore a white linen dress with ruffles on the end of each sleeve. She was even more beautiful than I remembered.

"Jane, you're a sight for sore eyes," I said playfully.

Jane blushed and looked toward Ricardo. He smiled at the both of us and then rose to give me a hug.

"I'm glad you're alright, old friend," he said. "But you can't have my lady."

We both laughed heartedly and Jane wiggled between us, placing one arm around the neck of Ricardo, the other around my own.

"Ricardo, I only have eyes for you, my sweet," she assured him. Then she looked at me with sparkling green eyes and gave me a light kiss on the cheek. "But Redd may have the rest of me," she said, a little too seductively.

I must have turned a dark shade of red because the two of them began roaring with laughter. I joined in the laughter, doing my best not to sound embarrassed. Jane finally let out a yawn, and let her head rest upon my shoulder.

"I am so tired," she said.

"So go to bed," Ricardo suggested.

"I can't," she replied sleepily.

"Why can't you?" Ricardo asked. "You had a long night. Go get some rest."

"Redd just got here," she replied, still resting her head upon my shoulder. "I can't go to bed now; it would be rude."

"No, it's quite alright," I chirped. "I know how busy the nights are for you here. By all means, do not let me keep you from your sleep."

She rose her head up and gave me a sweet look.

"Do not leave without saying goodbye to me," she commanded.

I smiled. "No, of course not. Get some sleep, lass," I said. "I'll still be around when you wake. I've got matters to discuss with Ricardo."

"Alright," she said, suddenly yawning again. She turned to Ricardo and kissed him hard on the lips.

The display of affection made me cringe as I'd almost forgotten that Ricardo was still standing there. Jane had the ability to enchant me that way and I silently cursed myself for letting my guard down. I hoped Ricardo didn't notice.

"She is a fine woman, yes?" Ricardo stated after she left the room.

"Aye, that she is," I replied.

"She is very fond of you, Redd. Always has been," Ricardo said. "Perhaps you should've pursued her yourself."

He eyed me closely to see how I'd react. The conversation was making me quite uncomfortable and when he realized this, Ricardo erupted in laughter.

"Señor, I am only teasing you—relax, my friend!"

I decided my best course of action was to laugh in return, but in truth there was nothing funny about any of it to me.

"Ricardo, there is an important matter I need to discuss with you." I looked around the crowded room. "Privately, if at all possible."

Ricardo led me to a staircase in a darkened corner of the dining hall. Once on the second level, I followed him through a doorway that led into a corridor with a great balcony attached. I approached the edge of the balcony and peered over the edge. I saw what I'd become accustomed to seeing in the vast fenced-in area behind Jane's kitchen.

Ricardo was a collector of large cats and it was here that he kept the menagerie of—at last count—thirteen animals, most of which were lions and tigers. His personal favorite, a massive lion named Samson, glared up at me with large yellow eyes from the grassy field below. The large cat was seated, its tail twitching slightly, and suddenly opened its large maw in a frightening yawn of white, pointy death. I shuddered at the sight.

"Have a seat, señor," Ricardo said, motioning toward a small round table with two cushioned chairs.

Once seated, I quickly caught him up on everything that had happened since I'd last seen him. I began with the meeting with Governor Winters and ended with the arrest of Gordon Littleton. I held back nothing regarding the signet ring in Captain Trimble's possession, for I knew that Ricardo was a believer in such things. I guessed that he would be more apt to help me if I included the magical elements of the story. My assumptions proved correct.

"The signet ring of King Solomon is a story I've heard of, and it surprises me that an Englishmen like yourself had not," Ricardo quipped.

"I'm not a well-educated man," I admitted. "However, the sea is something I *do* know, and I know of the frightening creatures that exist within its depths. No pirate I know of—and especially a vile scallywag such as Trimble—should have that sort of power at his disposal. The seas—no, the world—will be his! Men like you and me cannot sit idly by and let it happen!"

"And we won't," Ricardo growled, slamming his fist onto the table. "My men and I will assist you on this quest. I'm sure the *Sea Witch* has countless treasures within her as well as charts and maps that will lead us to more! My men will not cower at the name of Trimble if there is gold and jewels involved."

I could hardly contain my smile, but I managed to stifle one to keep the mood serious.

"It is not only your muscle and ships that I need, mate, but your mind as well,' I said.

Ricardo's eyes narrowed and his face twisted into an expression of bewilderment.

"My mind? I'm afraid I do not understand, señor," he replied.

"For me and my crew to complete this quest, in addition to you and your lot, I need your wits so that I may devise a plan to overtake the Royal Navy ship *Neptune's Castle.* I must rescue Gordon Littleton and take the ship as my own."

Ricardo sighed and for a moment I feared I'd asked too much of my old friend.

"What sort of ship is this *Neptune's Castle*?" he asked finally.

"English galleon," I replied. "Forty guns on her."

Ricardo nodded, his jaw clenched.

"Any treasure on board?"

I shook my head. "I do not believe that there is, but I am not sure," I answered.

"I see," he said, sounding somewhat disappointed with that. "Give me time to go and speak to my crew. I must get them behind me or they will be no good to us."

He rose from his chair and placed a reassuring hand on my shoulder.

"Wait here for a moment. I will go downstairs and speak to them now."

I nodded and tried to flash a confident smile. Suddenly, I felt a wave of anxiety wash over me as I thought of the possibility that his crew would be unanimously against the dangerous mission.

I waited for what seemed like an hour when I heard the sound of boot steps approaching from behind. I turned and as expected it was Ricardo, his face looking somewhat tired. This was not a good sign.

"Redd, my old friend," he began. "I'm afraid my news is both good and bad."

I cringed at that.

"Okay, give me the good news first," I said.

"They are all behind you in your quest to stop Captain Trimble. There was a boisterous sound of unity among the men and I was proud to see that they all were willing to shoulder such a burden for the fate of the world."

"And the bad news?" I asked reluctantly.

Ricardo pulled his hat from his head and laid it on the table before him; he drummed his fingers on the table.

"It seems that most of my crew is unwilling to help in your efforts to rescue Mr. Littleton."

I closed my eyes and turned my head in a pitiful attempt to hide my disappointment.

"Very well," I said, rising from the table. "You did what you could and I am quite pleased that you are all so willing to help with Captain Trimble."

Ricardo rose from the table, a shameful look upon his face.

"Redd, I consider Gordon a personal friend of mine," he said.

I held up a hand in what could only be construed as a rude attempt to silence him.

"Ricardo, it is alright and there is no reason to apologize. A captain must listen to the concerns of his crew and heed them as well."

"Yes," he replied. "But I am apologizing for nothing."

The comment struck me as if it were a slap on the face. I stared at him with wide-eyed surprise.

"Calm yourself," Ricardo said, sensing my building anger. "I said that *most* of my crew is unwilling to help, not *all* of them."

"Please get to the point," I said impatiently.

"You will have my sword, and the swords of all on my crew that are willing," he said, smiling. "We will probably be outmanned, but as you said earlier, it is not only my muscle that you need, but my wits as well."

"Aye, I did," I replied.

"Well, señor, I've already come up with a plan that I think will work so that we may save Gordon and make *Neptune's Castle* yours."

Chapter 8

Ricardo commanded a fleet of ships, but the prize of the lot was a Spanish galleon affectionately named *Jane*. She was quite a large ship, armed with fifty guns and usually crewed by close to 200 pirates. Her fearsome size sometimes proved to be problematic during battle, for a ship that size is not endowed with the maneuverability of a sloop or brig. Intimidation seemed to do the trick where smaller ships were concerned and, more times than not, Ricardo managed to overtake a foe without firing a single cannon. Most captains that piloted smaller ships were content to surrender and embrace their new lives instead of fighting or running and therefore chancing a trip to Davy Jones's locker.

Ricardo chose *Jane* for our well-planned confrontation with Captain Edward Sutton and *Neptune's Castle*; the former ship being slightly larger than the latter. It was his hope that the sheer size of the ship would give us a little added insurance when it came time to execute the devious plan we'd concocted on the balcony a short time ago.

Unfortunately, there would be no crew of 200 pirates, as it seemed only fifty of Ricardo's men decided to join my own crew of thirty-nine. Nevertheless, it would be enough men to pilot both *Jane* and *Henrietta*.

We spent what little of the afternoon remained loading *Jane* with food and water needed to continue onward to New Providence directly after our mission to acquire Gordon and *Neptune's Castle*.

That evening, when the ships were nearly ready to set sail, I returned to Jane's Kitchen and said goodbye to the establishment's namesake (as I'd promised). I would have liked a moment alone with her, but Ricardo accompanied me. I suppose it was his right to do so since Jane was his mate and not mine. However, his presence made me uncomfortable and made me feel as if I had to harness my emotions when I spoke to her. I admitted to myself that it was wrong of me to feel that way about my friend's lover, but it was not something within my control.

When we arrived, Jane was already hard at work in the kitchen, so much so that she did not even notice our presence. Ricardo tip-toed behind her and slipped his arms around her waist. She was obviously familiar with his touch, or maybe even the smell of him, because she smiled without even looking back. She knew it was him. Jane tilted her head back and kissed Ricardo on the lips. The gesture turned my insides into knots, but no one would be able to tell by looking at me. I made sure of it.

It was at this moment that Jane peered over at me. As my eyes met her sparkling green ones, it was all I could do to keep myself from smiling a boyish grin. It seemed my only defense was to simply look away from her. She took Ricardo to a private corner of the kitchen, and out of the corner of my eye I could see them whispering. From the look upon Jane's face, I figured out that Ricardo was telling her of our plan to hunt down Captain Trimble and the *Sea Witch*. When they finished speaking the two of them suddenly embraced as if it would be the last time they would ever see each other again. The thought of Jane never seeing Ricardo again gave my heart a flutter of hope—I suddenly shook my head and found myself feeling shame for even allowing a thought like that to enter my head.

The two of them finally strolled back in my direction, arm in arm. Once they were within an arm's reach of me, Jane pulled away from Ricardo and put her arms around my neck, pulling me down toward her. She kissed me on the cheek.

"I'll look after Ricardo," I said to her softly.

"I know that you will," she replied and then she pulled my ear close to her lips. "If anything should happen to him, I want you to be the one to tell me," she whispered.

I drew back from her and nodded in acknowledgement.

"Everything is going to be just fine, don't you worry," I assured her.

She nodded, but her somber expression told me she didn't believe me. Jane returned to her work, and we reluctantly left her to it.

Ricardo returned to his ship as I boarded *Henrietta*. Both of us said nothing as we parted ways, for we were focused on the mission. Upon my boarding, I was soon greeted by my anxious crew, all of them eager to hear my plans. I stepped upon the quarterdeck with Andrea to my right and Oliver Langley to my left. The rest of the men gathered down below on the waist, Robert Lynch standing attentively at the point.

I told them the plan that Ricardo and I had concocted on the upper balcony behind Jane's Kitchen and as I concluded the last detail, the men rallied together in a cry of support that made my heart swell with pride. Robert then began barking instructions to the crew as I instructed Langley to set a northeasterly course into the Windward Passage. Our heading was a tiny collection of islands due north of Tortuga and the southwestern most land masses of the Bahama Islands.

It was common for the Royal Navy and other ships traveling to Europe to pass near these islands. It was there that we planned to intercept Captain Sutton and *Neptune's Castle* before they disappeared into the vastness of the Atlantic Ocean.

I was thankful for the overwhelming support of my men, but that moment was short lived as I was soon reminded that there was a certain woman on board also.

"I do not like this plan, it's foolish and dangerous," Andrea snapped.

She was on my heels as I entered my cabin, and I was glad she at least waited to express her displeasure in private.

"Yes, sweetling, I suppose it is," I replied, taking a seat at the table. "Gordon said the same thing when I shared my plan with him to break you out of that prison carriage."

She couldn't help but smile at that, but she quickly regained her composure. I snatched up a bottle of rum off the table and yanked the cork free with my teeth. Andrea sat across from me, and I poured us both a mug full of the dark liquid.

"Captain, I suppose I have to admit that there is more courage in you than there is foolishness," she said, pausing to take a drink. She closed her eyes tightly and seemed to wince as she swallowed the mouthful of rum.

"That hit the spot, did it?" I asked, chuckling.

She held the back of her hand to her mouth and I could make out the corners of a wide smile behind it.

"I bet your father never made it like *that,* now did he?" I said. Then I took a big gulp of my own. It had never tasted better.

"No, he didn't," she said, once the initial shock subsided. "It should take me some time to become accustomed to that..." She paused, searching for a word. "Flavor," she said finally.

"You stay with this crew of scallywags and it shouldn't take long at all," I said. "Now, what of my plan? What don't you like about it?"

She cocked her head, genuinely confused by my question. "Oh, I don't know, maybe the part about the giant—"

"Captain!" Langley exclaimed as he barged in, interrupting the exchange. "Do I smell the sweet aroma of rum in here?"

"Aye, you do, mate," I replied, tossing him the bottle.

He caught it and immediately put the opening to his lips, then began to chug away. Andrea looked on in stunned disbelief. When he finally pulled the bottle from his mouth, he wiped the moisture from his lips and sighed with pleasure.

"Do you mind if scurry along with this, Cap'n?" he asked, pointing to the bottle.

"Not at all," I answered cheerfully. "I've got plenty more."

With that answer, Langley spun on his heel and retreated toward the quarterdeck.

Andrea looked at me and I stared back. Soon we both erupted into laughter.

"The trip to the Bahama Islands is a short one," she said, giggling. "If all goes according to plan, do you think he will be drunk enough by then to pilot a ship as large as *Neptune's Castle*?"

"I truly hope so," I replied, laughing still.

"Well, I still don't like this plan, but I support you none the less," she said. "I mean, what choice do I have?"

"None that I can see," I answered. "You will think it's a bloody good one when it works."

"Aye, and if it works, you'll receive my humble apology," she said.

"Keep your apology," I quipped. "That's too easy—I want you to truly feel remorse for doubting your captain."

She eyed me suspiciously.

"Well, what do you have in mind, my captain?"

"If all goes well, and I reclaim Gordon and that bloody ship, you will reward me with a kiss."

"Oh, I will?" she said, taken aback.

"Aye," I replied. "You sound worried, lass. If you're so sure I'll fail, what do you have to fear?"

"No, Captain," she argued. "I do not *want* you to fail because it's obviously in all of our best interests for you to succeed. But I'll play your little game, and if you should succeed, I will reward you with a kiss."

"Very well," I said, satisfied with the arrangement.

"But don't you think for a second that I'll enjoy the bloody moment," she added quickly. "As a matter of fact, you had better go ahead and give me another bottle of that rum so I'll be in such a condition to go through with it."

***

We arrived at our destination just as the sun was beginning to rise from the eastern sky. I stood upon the quarterdeck; the pleasant sensation of the cool morning breeze washed over my face. I took a deep breath of the fresh morning air and set my gaze toward the heavens. There were still plenty of stars visible, and a sliver of moon accompanied them. The sea was eerily calm and I regarded that as a good omen. It seemed as of late that I was becoming more and more the superstitious type. The last few days had undoubtedly taken a toll on me, both physically and mentally. I didn't feel that I'd gotten a good night's rest since my last night at sea aboard *Rebecca*. That was days ago, but it felt more like weeks. The thought forced me into a long yawn.

"You should take a moment to rest, Cap'n," a familiar voice called out from the waist below me.

It was Jolly Jack. Unbeknownst to me, he'd been watching me and could see the obvious fatigue setting in.

"No time for rest, Jack," I replied wearily. "The next few hours are going to be a bit hairy. When the sails of *Neptune's Castle* are spotted, the last thing I should be doing is napping."

"Aye, Cap'n," he said, then paused as if he contemplated arguing the issue further. I decided to give him an order so he wouldn't have to.

"Jack, raise the colors," I said quickly.

"Aye" was the only reply, and he disappeared below deck to fetch the Union Flag.

I decided the best way to remain awake and alert would be for me to take a stroll throughout the ship so that I may get an idea of the morale of the crew. I spotted Joe swabbing the deck along with a few of the other former slaves. They scrubbed the timber in such a fashion that gave me an idea about the sort of slave owner they'd been unfortunate enough to serve under. The deck had quickly become the cleanest I'd ever seen and yet the men polished it further as if they feared some sort of cruel punishment would await them if someone noticed they had stopped. I strolled to them and stood near Joe.

"Joe, may I have a moment?" I asked.

Joe stood abruptly, the mop still clutched firmly in his right hand.

"Yes sir, what do you need?" he replied without missing a beat.

I gently grabbed his arm and led him to a more private area, near the port-side railing.

"Joe, you and your men are doing a fine job," I said.

He smiled.

"Thank you, sir, that's mighty kind of you to say," he replied, his teeth gleaming brightly. "We do our best to earn our keep."

"Well you're certainly doing that," I assured him. "However, I must admit that there is a slight problem."

He frowned at that, and I swear the man looked as if he were on the verge of tears.

"Relax, Joe," I said quickly. "I said the problem is *slight*."

That seemed to make him ease up a bit, but I could still feel the tension radiate from him.

"Listen closely because the words I'm about to speak have never crossed my lips before and most certainly never will again," I stated matter-of-factly.

Joe's eyes narrowed and he bit his lip with anticipation.

"Joe, as I said, you and your friends are doing a fine job," I repeated. "However, I've paid quite a bit of attention to you all, and it seems to me that you're working a tad too hard, mate."

Joe's mouth dropped open, and his eyes followed suit, rolling toward the floor. At first, I thought it was an expression of dejection, but quickly realized it instead was genuine bewilderment. After a moment, he looked back up at me, a blank stare etched on his face.

"We're working *too* hard, Cap'n?" he asked, dumbfounded.

I couldn't help but laugh at his childlike innocence. I placed a hand upon his shoulder and squeezed gently.

"Joe, what I'm trying to say is that I would like to see you and the other men take breaks every now and then. Explore the ship and befriend your shipmates." I spread my arms out. "This is your new family and the sea is your new home. Learn everything you can about all of it," I said. "You can't do that if you spend every waking moment swabbing the bloody deck, now can you?"

He took a long look at his surroundings and allowed my suggestion to sink in for a moment. Finally, his gaze rested on me and his expression was serious.

"Captain, we will do as you wish, but please understand that this is not a life we are accustomed to just yet," he said. "It will take some time for us to become comfortable taking these... *breaks* you are suggesting. If you notice that we are resting too much, please let us know."

He said the word "breaks" as if it was a dirty word. It was hard for me to imagine what I was quickly beginning to understand. Ever since they'd been boys, these men had done practically nothing but manual labor from sun up to sun down.

"Very well," I replied. "Just make sure you use the time to explore the ship and to become familiar with the crew and all will be well."

Joe nodded and even allowed himself a small grin. Then he returned to his work. I considered ordering all of them to put down the bloody mops right that instant, but thought better of it. I left them to their work and decided I would observe them later to see how well they followed my orders.

A few hours later, the sun shone brightly and the pleasant morning began the transition into a muggy, quite unpleasant noon. When *Henrietta* finally reached the tiny southernmost chain of

Bahamas, we dropped her anchor and awaited a few moments for the *Jane* to glide along our port side.

The Spanish men aboard *Jane* quickly threw their grappling irons onto the railing of *Henrietta* and then began to pull her near them. Once the two ships connected, Ricardo stepped aboard my ship.

"How is your… cargo?" I asked him.

"Quite calm for now," he replied with an easy smile. "I won't begin to worry until we close those crates up."

"How are you going to keep them closed?"

"I decided it would be best to tie the lids of the crates down with rope, that way if things begin to go badly, one slash of my cutlass will render them free."

I glanced up at the mainmast of *Jane* to make sure the Jolly Roger was flying as it should be. It was, and then I set my sights upon my own mainmast to reassure myself that the royal colors were flying above my own ship. So far, everything was going according to plan. Yet somehow, I could not deny an uneasy feeling that began to build deep inside me. I'd experienced that uneasy feeling before and it usually preceded a series of unfortunate events. I'd learned to rely a lot on that feeling over the years, and now I was trying to force myself to ignore it. I suppose I didn't have much of a choice in the matter. This was my only shot at getting Gordon back and possibly getting a ship that would suffice my needs all at the same time. It was now or never and there was no time for feelings of doubt now.

"Sail ho!"

The cry originated from the crow's nest of *Jane*, and suddenly my worried feelings were replaced with a wave of anxiety. Ricardo perked up at the sound, and he rushed up the stairs to the quarterdeck. He did not stop until he reached the stern and it was there that he retrieved a looking glass. He held the glass to his eye and pointed it toward the horizon behind us. I heard him let out a nervous sigh and then he passed the glass to me.

I focused the round picture ahead until I could make out the bright white tops of square sails.

"That's got to be them," I said softly, handing the looking glass back to Ricardo.

"Aye, it is time to get into position," he replied.

With that, Ricardo sprinted back to his own ship and began barking orders to his crew. The men responded by scurrying below deck to retrieve the important cargo. Seven massive crates were already lined up on the waist of *Jane*. Six of them were missing lids as they awaited the cargo Ricardo's men had gone below deck to retrieve. The seventh was already sealed up; the two ropes wrapped around each end made it so.

"Should we get into position now?" Robert asked me suddenly.

I set my gaze upon the horizon again to check on the progress *Neptune's Castle* had made.

"Not yet," I replied. "We still have over half an hour before they will be able to see what is going on here."

"Aye Captain, I will gather all of the men on deck and await your orders," Robert said.

I rushed back down the steps to take a peek into my cabin. As expected, Andrea was still sedated quite heavily from the vast quantities of rum she'd consumed the night before. I knew she would've wanted to be involved in the day's mission, but I couldn't risk her being spotted by one of Captain Sutton's crew. A woman aboard the ship would have raised suspicion. Furthermore, Andrea was vital to make sure that my eventual goal of finding Trimble was reached. I could not—would not—risk losing her. So I decided the best course of action would be to get her as drunk as possible so that I may remove her from the situation altogether.

I scooped her up into my arms and lifted her off the bed. She let out a little whimper in response but remained asleep. I carried her out onto the deck and whistled at Langley who stood above me on the quarterdeck behind. The sound startled him and he peered down at me.

"Langley, grab the keys and meet me at the brig," I ordered him.

He arrived at the brig mere moments after I did and he quickly used the keys to open the iron door. Langley arranged Andrea's coat in such a way to create a makeshift pillow for her. I gently laid her on the floor of the brig, resting her head upon the coat. I then took her hat and situated it atop her head in a fashion that would hide the majority of her face. I then stepped out of the iron cage and locked the door behind, taking a moment to take another look at her before I left. She looked very much like she did the first time I ever saw her and just as the first time I'd ever saw her, she appeared more like a boy instead of a woman. If Captain Sutton decided to search my ship, he'd assume she was nothing more than a lad that had drunk too much and was sleeping it off. That was the story I'd give him anyway.

Langley and I returned to the quarterdeck, and once again I set my sights upon the horizon to check on the progress of Captain Sutton and *Neptune's Castle*. The ship was clearly trimming distance now, and I estimated she'd broadside us in less than twenty minutes. I looked over toward *Jane* again and was relieved to see them putting the last of their cargo into the final crate.

Ricardo, along with ten of his men, returned to our ship. It was time to begin the charade.

"Robert, get the men into position," I said.

Robert gave the command and all of the men formed a line, each of them sitting with their backs against the starboard railing. Once Langley and I joined them, Ricardo and his men rested their hands upon the hilts of their cutlasses and waited for *Neptune's Castle* to arrive.

"I sure hope this works," Langley grumbled under his breath.

Ricardo had known Oliver Langley even longer than I, and he laughed at his old friend's worried tone.

"Have faith, señor," Ricardo said with a chuckle. "My plan will not fail us."

I leaned forward and looked at the faces of my crew. Most of the men seemed calm and collected. Ironically, the only men who seemed somewhat anxious were the two largest men on the ship. Hale Woodrow, the ship's carpenter, seemed to fidget quite a bit with his hands and stare at the deck. Joe closed his eyes and his lips moved as if he were praying silently to himself.

I smiled at both of the gentle giants and did not let their moods concern me. I knew that if a battle broke out, both of them would probably be the most dangerous men on the ship. Men that feared death would do everything in their power to avoid it. Fortunately for Joe and Hale, they both possessed quite a bit of power in their large frames. It was a dangerous combination, and I was glad to have them both on my side.

"Alright, señores," Ricardo whispered. "The ship is here… it is time to play our little game."

It was at that moment he unsheathed his cutlass.

Chapter 9

As the large ship glided closer, the first thing I noticed about her was the beautiful wooden figure on the bowsprit. The carved face was that of an older man with a full head of hair and a beard to match. His eyes were squinted and his thick eyebrows suggested an expression of anger. A mighty trident was clutched tightly in the figure's right hand, and his body was that of a young, strong man. The Greeks called the man Poseidon, god of the sea. The Romans referred to him as Neptune.

I'd seen *Neptune's Castle* briefly before I'd left Port Royal, but it was from a great distance. This was the first good look I'd gotten of her, and she was even more magnificent than I had originally thought. Much of her hull boasted a wide stripe of light blue paint, trimmed with gold. The stripe ran across the gun ports, which I quickly noticed were already opened. The black tips of twelve-pounder cannons protruded from the openings. It was obvious that Captain Sutton had already pieced together the dire situation that Ricardo and I were trying to depict. To him, *Henrietta* was a sloop under duress from a much larger pirate ship. To make the matter more personal, *Henrietta* proudly displayed the Union colors upon her main mast. Ricardo's ship flew a black flag, and once Sutton discovered the *Jane* was crewed by *Spanish* pirates... well, that would just add fuel to the proverbial fire.

"Pirates, under the authority of King George I command you to drop your weapons at once," a voice, that I could only assume belonged to Captain Sutton, boomed from the speaking trumpet held at his lips.

"I don't think so, señor," Ricardo yelled in response. "Be on your way, or I'll paint these decks with English blood."

Ricardo then slapped a hand across Langley's forehead and pulled his head backward so that his stubbly throat arched outward. He then placed the blade he wielded against Langley's throat. I noticed Langley's Adam's apple nervously bobbing up and down. I couldn't tell if the reaction was for show, or if he was genuinely scared. The blade was clearly against Langley's throat—

Ricardo was putting on a very convincing performance and I couldn't help but feel a twinge of uncertainty.

There was a long pause before Sutton spoke again.

"Pull that blade away from that man's throat," he said finally. His tone was neither weak nor commanding. "I do not want to see any blood spilled today. Let us make an effort to negotiate."

Ricardo relaxed a little and released the tension on Langley's head. He continued to hold the blade close to his throat, but the steel no longer made contact with skin.

"Very smart, señor," Ricardo said. "I am willing to negotiate as long as it does not include surrendering… I would rather die."

"You seem to be a very desperate man, and I take you for your word." Captain Sutton responded. "However, you must understand my predicament. You are standing on an English ship, threatening to murder innocent men—English men. My vessel has twenty guns ready to rain death upon you the moment you draw a drop of blood from your hostages."

Ricardo grinned, and then released a hearty cackle.

"Señor, I thought I made myself very clear," he shouted back. "I would rather die than surrender today. No one has to die unless you make it so! Allow me to return to my ship and I will set these men free."

"Where is the captain of that ship?" Sutton barked in reply.

Ricardo hesitated, then abruptly grabbed my shoulder and forced me to stand. Once I was on my feet, I was finally able to get a good look at the captain of *Neptune's Castle*.

Captain Edward Sutton was a tall man and built like a bull. Tufts of dark brown hair could be seen escaping the confines of the royal blue bicorn hat that adorned his head. Sutton's brown hair was so dark, it almost looked black—and as I studied it closer, I suppose it could have been. The most striking feature was his eyes… they were almost as dark as his hair, and his eyebrows matched. Captain Sutton's piercing eyes were intimidating and impossible to gaze upon for a long length of time.

Those frightening eyes were now locked on me and as Sutton studied me for a long moment, I noticed another man standing beside him. When the other man caught sight of me, his expression seemed to indicate that he recognized me. Then he suddenly leaned over and whispered something to Captain Sutton. The mystery man seemed familiar to me also, though I couldn't place where I'd seen him. The fact that I never got a complete view of his entire face didn't help matters. The mystery man recognizing me was troubling, but Ricardo and I had also considered that possibility. It truly did not matter if the entire ship recognized me at this point and, truth be told, it may help with our deception. Regardless of what the men aboard *Neptune's Castle* thought of me, the fact remained that I was on urgent business from Governor Winters, and all they knew was that a Spanish pirate ship was hindering me from my task.

"Captain, have any of your men been harmed?" Sutton asked me with genuine concern.

I shook my head.

"No sir, not yet," I replied.

"Allow me to have a moment to speak with the captain," Sutton asked Ricardo.

"So speak to him, señor," Ricardo replied nonchalantly. "I am not stopping you."

"I would prefer to speak to the captain alone," Captain Sutton responded, clearly irritated with the cocky pirate.

"And why would I allow that?" Ricardo asked.

"A sign of good faith," he responded. "Allow me this favor and I may consider allowing you and your men to go free. You may stay aboard the ship with your hostages until I return with the captain. By then I will have decided your fate."

Ricardo stared at Captain Sutton for a long moment as if he were trying to burn a hole through the man. It was all part of the show, I knew; however, he played his role so well that I had to remind myself that he was actually on my side.

"I will allow you to take a moment alone with the captain," he said finally. "All the while, I will be deciding *your* fate as well, señor."

"Very well," Sutton conceded. "Send him aboard at once."

Once I was on board *Neptune's Castle* I had a much better look at the mystery man that had been speaking with Captain Sutton. I instantly recognized him and once I realized who he was, I immediately felt my pulse quicken.

The man was the governor's nephew, Augustus Flynn. My last encounter with him did not go well and I feared that I was about to experience more of the same.

I took a seat at the beautiful mahogany table in Captain Sutton's cabin while Flynn and other officers whom I did not recognize joined me.

"Welcome aboard, pirate," Flynn hissed. He glared at me with pure hatred and for a moment I was afraid that the plan Ricardo and I had concocted was on the verge of coming apart.

"Augustus, that's enough," Captain Sutton said sternly. "Captain Reeves is not a pirate. At the present time he is a privateer on an urgent mission for the governor."

Sutton grabbed a silver goblet off the table and took a gulp of wine. Flynn crossed his arms and clenched his jaw.

"Now tell me, Captain Reeves," Sutton continued. "No one knows anything about this mission Governor Winters has sent you and your men on. Are the Spanish involved in some way? Are they trying to stop you?"

"No," I said quickly. "The Spanish pirates have pursued us since we passed Tortuga. They began firing warning shots at us that got closer and closer until I feared they would sink us if we didn't drop anchor. They demanded that we give up any gold we have on board, but as I've been trying to tell the wretches, we have none. Captain, the mission I am undertaking is secret, and I swore an oath that I would keep the details secret."

Captain Sutton leaned back in his chair as he listened to me speak, he nodded and seemed to respect my position regarding the top-secret mission.

"I see," he replied. "So, you aren't carrying *any* gold?"

"No captain, we are not," I answered quickly. "The task Governor Winters has given me has nothing to do with gold."

"Lies," Flynn hissed abruptly. "These pirates are probably working together and I wouldn't be surprised if *both* of their ships are filled with gold."

"You're welcome to search my ship," I snapped at Flynn. "You will find no gold. As for the pirates, I wouldn't know what they're carrying since I've never met them before. As your captain just told you, I'm now a privateer sailing under the crown."

I reached for a silver goblet full of wine in front of me; but Flynn angrily slapped it away before I could touch it.

"Lies! Everything you're saying is lies, pirate!"

The contents of the flying goblet showered over two of the officers seated at the end of the table. They immediately rose from their seats, both of them wet and shaking with rage.

"Augustus, that temper of yours is going to be the death of you," Captain Sutton's voice boomed loudly. "Get out of my cabin at once! I will deal with your stupidity later."

Flynn glared at me with more of his increasingly familiar hatred. He then peered around the room at the other officers seated at the table and finally to the two older gentlemen he'd doused with wine.

"Very well," he said finally.

He then stormed out the room, slamming the door so hard that I thought the glass would shatter from the cabin windows.

"I apologize for Augustus's behavior," Sutton said. "If his uncle was not the governor, he'd be locked away in the brig right now."

The captain shifted in his chair.

"I understand that the two of you have had a recent conflict," he said.

"We had a—disagreement regarding the arrest of a member of my crew," I said reluctantly. Discussing Gordon Littleton was not the direction I wanted the conversation to head. I knew that Ricardo and the others were counting on me to keep things moving according to plan.

"Ah, you're speaking of the murderer Gordon Littleton," Sutton said as if he were reading my mind. "The same Gordon Littleton that is now locked up in the brig of this very ship."

"Aye," I replied. "That's the one. However, please understand, Captain Sutton, that Gordon is the least of my worries now. He is locked away safely below your decks while the rest of my crew has swords pointed at their backs."

Captain Sutton eyed me suspiciously for a long moment before finally nodding.

"Yes, I suppose we need to discuss how to deal with this unfortunate situation," he replied. "What can you tell me about those pirates?"

"I can tell you that you have them severely outmanned," I said quickly. "I can also tell you that they're prepared to buy their freedom from you," I added.

The captain's eyes grew bigger.

"They're prepared to *buy* their freedom?" he repeated, awestruck. "How do you know this?"

"I know it because I learned to speak Spanish as a child," I replied. "The pirate captain has been conversing with officers on his crew regarding how they would deal with you and yours as soon as they spotted this ship's sails. They were already on board my ship when they finally spotted you and there wasn't enough time to get their large ship away. The captain ordered the crew to bring up several large crates filled with treasure to the main deck for the sole purpose of bribing you so that they may escape. Of course, I do not believe that they are keen on giving up *all* of their gold, but they seemed desperate enough to do it if it was their last resort."

Captain Sutton drummed his fingers on the mahogany table as he considered all I'd said. He seemed to be struggling with how to deal with the situation.

"No," he said abruptly.

"No?" I asked, trying not to sound panicked.

"I will cut them all down and take their gold too," he replied with a sinister grin. "I will not allow freedom to be bought by pirates."

My heart began to sink as the gravity of the situation began to weigh heavily upon me. I felt certain that the captain would avoid fighting if he believed he'd receive vast quantities of gold.

"Captain, may I give you my humble opinion?" one of the older officers suddenly chimed in. He looked to be in his late fifties or early sixties. His vision appeared to be poor as evidenced by his glazed look. In short, this was a man who had no business on a Royal Navy ship. Yet here he was, and I could only hope that the seemingly wise old man's opinion would be one that helped my cause.

"Why of course, Harry," Captain Sutton replied in a tone that suggested he valued the older man's advice.

"I believe it would be wise to acquire the treasure and *then* attack the pirates while they *think* they are escaping. If you refuse their offer and a battle breaks out, then the treasure could be lost if it sinks with their ship."

Captain Sutton leaned back in his chair and crossed his arms. He smiled widely.

"And that is why Harry has been my most trusted advisor," he said, looking at me. "Very well, let us return to deck and negotiate a bargain with these pirates."

I could see the relief on Ricardo's face when we returned to deck and I hoped that Captain Sutton didn't pick up on it. It soon became apparent that he had not when he began shouting at Ricardo.

"Pirate, I've decided that there will be no negotiating! Surrender at once or meet your certain death, the choice is yours!"

Ricardo held an icy gaze on Captain Sutton, and I knew he was hiding a great feeling of relief. It was obvious that he realized we had the captain right where we wanted him. As I expected, Ricardo returned his cutlass to its scabbard and kept our plan moving forward.

"Señor," he began with a chuckle. "I had a feeling you would come back and say something like that. As I told you, I'm just not in the surrendering mood today, but I have a proposition that I believe will make us both happy and everyone can keep their heads too."

"I'm listening, but be quick about it," Captain Sutton replied smugly. He glanced over at me and allowed a cocky grin.

"I've got more treasure on my ship than you can imagine," Ricardo answered. "I will be willing to part with some of it if you allow me and my men to sail away unharmed."

"You will be willing to part with *some* of it, pirate?" Sutton replied. "Sorry, but I'm not interested. I think I'll just blow holes in your ship and help myself to *all* of it instead."

Ricardo rolled his eyes for dramatic effect.

"All right, all right," he shouted. "You can have it all! Just allow me and my men to leave unmolested."

Ricardo pulled off the act beautifully, and he seemed genuinely desperate to escape the dire situation he found himself in.

Captain Sutton leaned on the railing of *Neptune's Castle* and gazed into the water lapping gently between the two ships. He seemed to be considering Ricardo's offer, and it seemed ironic to me that suddenly he and Ricardo were both acting out emotions that neither of them truly felt. When Captain Sutton decided he'd pretended to ponder the offer long enough, he then continued his own act.

"Very well," he barked. "You and your men begin moving all of the treasure on board my ship at once, but be quick about it. This little excursion has put me and my crew behind schedule."

"The treasure you are about to receive will make it worth your while, señor," Ricardo replied in his most relieved voice.

He then began barking instructions to the crew still on board *Jane*. The men began to fashion a series of ropes and pulleys to transport the heavy crates from *Jane* to *Neptune's Castle*.

When the first crate arrived on board his ship, Captain Sutton used his cutlass to cut the binding ropes. He then pulled the lid free and his eyes widened as the sparkling treasure gleamed brightly in the midday sun.

"It is beautiful," he beamed proudly.

He then turned to the officers nearby and ordered them to begin the process of transporting each crate below deck as it came aboard.

"It seems you will be on your way in a matter of moments," he told me cheerfully. "Thank you for making me aware of this treasure. King George will be pleased."

"Aye, I'm sure that he will," I replied. "Put in a good word for me to his majesty when you see him."

Captain Sutton laughed at that and nodded.

When the seventh crate was safely below deck, Captain Sutton shouted at Ricardo to get his ship out of his sight.

"Aye, señor, it's been a pleasure doing business with you," the Spanish pirate replied.

"We're not finished yet," I heard Sutton whispered through clenched teeth.

He then turned to me and his mood changed.

"Come, captain," he said. "Let us examine the other crates of treasure and give those pirates time to shove off before I blast them out of the water."

"Thank you, captain," I replied. "But I'm behind schedule. I should return to my ship and see to my distraught crew."

Captain Sutton seemed disappointed but understanding of my position. He held out his hand and I quickly shook it.

"I appreciate your help," I said.

"Likewise, captain," he replied. "Steer clear of pirates for the duration of your mission, and it is my hope that you complete the governor's task without any future delays."

"Aye" was my only reply.

It was the last thing I'd ever say to the good captain and the last time I would ever see him alive.

I climbed back on board *Henrietta* where Robert and Langley had the rest of the crew already prepared for battle. The only thing to do now was wait for the screams. It didn't take long.

Captain Sutton had, as expected, wasted no time cutting the ropes loose on the other six crates. Unfortunately for him, there was no treasure to be found in the other crates. The first crate was only filled with genuine treasure to sell the act. When Sutton examined that first crate, the gold gleaming in his eyes was enough to make him believe the other crates contained the same. That mistake turned out to be the death of him. For when the other ropes that secured the other six crates were cut loose, the lions and tigers inside them were released. The bloody chaos that followed was our cue to board and finish the job.

Ricardo and his men heard the chilling screams also, and they promptly used the same rope and pulley system that transported the lions and tigers over to *Neptune's Castle* as their own avenue to storm the decks.

Robert, Langley and I led the crew of *Henrietta* aboard *Neptune's Castle*, and while the lions and tigers belonging to Ricardo handled most the crew below the decks, my crew, along with Ricardo's, clashed steel with members of the Royal Navy still remaining on the top decks.

I had already cut down two unlucky swabs when I heard someone angrily shout my name from somewhere above on the poop deck. I turned around to find none other than Augustus Flynn charging at me from above. I was in a most vulnerable position from where I stood on the waist and Flynn leapt at me from the deck above in an effort to cut me down with one quick blow. Had he not shouted at me first, he very well may have succeeded. Instead, I ducked low as he sailed past, the tip of his sword nicking my ear in the process. I scrambled to my feet and he did too, just as quickly. With the chaos continuing around us of pirates and redcoats battling with cutlasses and pistols alike, we began our own inevitable duel. Flynn, though young and energetic, was also quite clumsy with his swordsmanship. He came at me swinging his blade wildly in wide swaths, and when that failed to make contact he grabbed the hilt with both hands and charged at me with the weapon held above his head as if he were about to attack me with an axe. This unbridled rage caught me by surprise, and I could do nothing but roll out of the way to avoid the wild attack. Flynn stopped at the railing and reeled around at me, his blond hair becoming disheveled and his eyes burning with familiar rage.

Flynn charged at me, and again the wide, wild swaths of his sword approached, but this time I was prepared. My steel met his, and then I kicked him hard in the stomach. He fell backward; the railing on the ship was the only thing that kept him from falling.

"Flynn, I do not want to kill you," I told him, and I truly meant it. I was going to have enough problems with the Royal Navy when it was discovered that I stole their ship. I certainly didn't need the death of the governor's nephew on my head as well. "You have a chance to live, Flynn! Put your weapon down and climb aboard the *Henrietta* and no harm will come to you!"

I could see him clench his teeth and his eyes narrowed, unleashing his evil gaze upon me again. It was at that moment I knew there would be no way to avoid killing him. As expected, he resumed his wild attack, and again I was ready. My steel caught his again, and after a brief exchange of sword combat I found the opportunity I was looking for. Flynn couldn't resist the urge to go for a death blow on nearly every attack and, unfortunately for him, this made him very vulnerable. It was in one of those vulnerable moments that I planted the tip of my sword into his chest and then thrust the steel forward almost to the hilt.

Flynn immediately dropped his weapon and slumped forward; I caught him and quickly pulled my blade out of his heart. Blood gushed from the wound and Flynn grabbed at his chest in a futile effort to stop the bleeding. When it was apparent that his life was about to end, he peered into my eyes for a final time. The rage was gone, completely replaced by fear. I pitied him in that moment. He died in my arms and I laid him gently on the deck.

When I rose to my feet, the battle was over. The only men that survived the lions and tigers below deck were the ones that managed to escape through portholes and plunge into the ocean. They were fished out of the sea and grouped with the other men who were smart enough to surrender, all of which now found themselves the crew aboard *Henrietta*. When it was all over, only twenty-two men remained of the 150-man crew of *Neptune's Castle*.

As far as our casualties, I lost two of my own men. One was a young man named Jeff. I'd barely gotten to know the lad, and I felt some guilt about that. I knew that he'd been close to Jolly Jack and frequently helped him with the cooking. The other man was one of the former slaves whom I'd not gotten to know at all. I found Joe holding the man's lifeless body, tears streaming down his face. I placed a hand on his shoulder and tried to offer some words of comfort. I don't even remember what I said; it all felt like a dream. Whatever it was, it seemed to help because Joe nodded and the tears began to dry. Ricardo did not lose a single man, and part of me was envious of his good fortune.

After allowing Ricardo and some of his men time to capture and restrain the wild cats, I went below deck to see the carnage for myself. It was horrifying. There were mangled bodies everywhere, and now it was up to me and my men to clean it up.

I made my way to the brig where I found Gordon, his eyes big as saucers, no doubt a result of the horrifying scene that unfolded around him. When he saw me, I thought that he would burst into tears from sheer relief.

"Redd!" he shouted. "I should have known this was your work!"

I found a ring of keys hanging on a nearby wall and I promptly released him. He smiled and held out his hand which I immediately shook.

"I don't know what to say, captain," he said. "You came after me."

"Thank you is a good start," I replied. "I've got a job to do and I can't do it without you. Welcome back."

I noticed a mop leaned against the wall and I snatched it up and held it out to Gordon.

"What's this for?" he asked, bewildered.

"You're standing on our new ship, and as you can see," I looked around at the gore around us, "we've got some cleaning up to do and our time is quite short."

Gordon frowned and took the mop, but he made no attempt to argue. He immediately began to help with the cleanup efforts.

Hours later, we completed the gruesome task, and as I dropped the lifeless body of Captain Sutton over the side of *Neptune's Castle*, I felt as if the men I'd lost to the Royal Navy days ago were now avenged.

At some point during the cleanup, Andrea regained consciousness from the brig aboard *Henrietta*. Langley heard her screaming demands to be released and he promptly obliged. She then stormed aboard *Neptune's Castle* to find me. I'd just stepped upon the quarterdeck to address the crew when she arrived.

She immediately unleashed a barrage of insults, most of which I didn't even notice because I was too exhausted. It did anger me that she was lashing out in front of the entire crew, but again, I was simply too tired to care.

"It's nice to see you again too," I said with a forced smile.

"Although I don't agree with your decision to exclude me, I am grateful for the fact that you somehow managed to pull this off," she said, climbing the steps to join me on the quarterdeck.

When she finally arrived at my side, she abruptly and rather forcefully grabbed the back of my head, pulling my face to hers. Our lips connected, and she kissed me long and hard. The men all watched the comical display, and then they erupted in boisterous applause and whistles.

"That's the kiss you were promised," she said after releasing me.

I smiled at her and suddenly forgot about the insults that occurred seconds earlier.

"It's nice to see you are a woman that keeps her promises," I said.

I then returned my attention to the crew; it took a moment for the laughter and banter to die down after the surprise kiss.

"Alright, you scallywags, lend me your ears now," I ordered them, and the ruckus finally began to dissipate.

"You all fought bravely and I cannot thank you enough for your efforts. Although the taste of victory is quite sweet," I paused and scanned the crowd until I locked eyes with Joe, "there still lingers a bitter taste as well. We lost two men today... may we never forget their faces. When we fight on in the future, think of those men and fight for them. We've still got a monumental task ahead of us mates. It will take a lot more than lions and tigers to defeat Captain Trimble and the crew of the *Sea Witch*."

I paused another moment to let that sink in.

"However," I continued, "we've increased our odds significantly by acquiring this impressive ship we now stand upon. *Neptune's Castle* is ours, mates!"

The men roared and applauded.

"Our heading is New Providence and I promise you that once we are sailing, the rest of the evening will be spent celebrating our victory."

"Hop to it, you scurvy dogs!" Oliver Langley cried out. "There's a fresh bottle of rum calling my name, and I don't like to keep my friends waiting. Let's get this girl in the wind at once!"

With that, all the men scrambled to their stations and prepared to set sail. I jogged across the deck and then shimmied down a rope that ended on the main deck of *Henrietta*. Ricardo and his men had just finished tearing the sails and rigging off the ship's masts.

"This old lady won't be taking these men anywhere fast," he told me, and then he drew near so only I could hear him. "Are you sure you want to leave these men alive? It will take some time, but they will eventually name you as the responsible party for the deaths of many of their mates."

"Aye, I know they will," I agreed. "But I've never been keen on killing men that surrender, and I am not going to start now."

I took a moment to look over the pitiful lot of defeated sailors. They were bloody, and their hands were tied behind their backs. They'd lost many of their comrades, but despite all of that, they were alive.

"*Henrietta* is dead in the water," I added thoughtfully. "We'll leave them tied up and just before I shove off, I'll throw a knife on the deck. It'll take them some time, but one of them will eventually get to it and find a way to get free."

It was at that moment another idea occurred to me. I knew the men were listening to our conversation and I decided to use that to my advantage.

"Besides," I continued, "by the time these blokes get free, we'll be halfway to Madagascar."

Ricardo quickly picked up on my ploy and immediately joined in the lie.

"Aye, I hope you're right… these redcoats are quite crafty," he added. "There's a lot of water between here and Africa."

"That there is," I agreed with a wink. "We'd better set sail at once. I'll meet you at our next destination."

"See you there, mate," Ricardo replied, and with that we both returned to our rightful ships.

Once I was standing safely on the decks of *Neptune's Castle*, as promised, I threw a somewhat dull dagger onto the deck of *Henrietta*. The weapon wasn't in the vicinity of any of the tied-up sailors, but with a little coordinated effort, they would be able to reach it eventually.

I stood at the helm of my new ship and took the wheel in my hands. I wanted to be the first to take control of her. I gazed out across the vast sea ahead of me and marveled at the large golden sun setting on the horizon off to the west.

Once the ship was moving, I inhaled the cool, fresh breeze that was currently caressing my face in a different light. The sweet air was a wonderful reminder that somehow, I was still alive. I'd cheated death so many times over the past few days, I wondered how much longer it would be before my luck ran out. There was still much more to accomplish, and things were not going to get any easier.

Gordon appeared from below deck and came up the stairs to stand by my side. There was a long period that neither of us said anything. It seemed Gordon was having thoughts similar to my own.

"William, I will find a way to repay you for what you did for me today," he finally said in a somber tone.

"Gordon, the way I see it, I was repaying you," I replied.

He stared at me, confused.

"Well, I *did* force you into piracy," I explained. "You certainly didn't volunteer that day we met."

Gordon smiled at that and nodded his head in agreement.

"I suppose you're right about that," he said. "It was not a life I wanted at the time; however, I grew to embrace it. I just sort of accepted it as punishment for what I did to my wife and her lover."

"Do you have regrets?" I asked.

"Every day," Gordon replied. "It was a terrible thing that I did."

"Aye, but it was a terrible thing your wife did to you as well," I reminded him.

He looked at me, a shameful look upon his face.

"She still didn't deserve to die," he said. "I allowed jealous rage to take over and the next thing I knew, they were both dead. I wish I could take it back, but of course I can't. Because of that fact, I have embraced my life as a pirate, and I will do all that I can to make the most of it. Men like you and Oliver make the journey somewhat easier."

I could almost feel the pain Gordon was feeling, and it made me pity him. I reached over and put a firm hand on his shoulder.

"I'm glad to have you on my crew," I told him. "But please know that you are free to go any time you like."

He smiled as he stared at the setting sun.

"I know that, William," he replied. "I do not want to go. This is my life now and if I try to live it any other way it just wouldn't feel right."

He took in a deep breath of ocean air.

"Now," he continued. "Enough about the past; I assume you're still hell bent on chasing down Captain Trimble."

"Aye," I replied. "And I assume you're still with me?"

"Of course," Gordon said. "I'm not going anywhere."

Jolly Jack suddenly scrambled up the stairs from below deck with a familiar scrap of black cloth bundled in his arms.

"Cap'n, I think it's time to hoist this ship's true colors," he said, shaking the bundled black cloth out to reveal an image of a white skeleton with a red skull holding a cutlass.

"I agree, Jack," I replied. "Hoist the Jolly Roger and there it shall remain until a better pirate rips it from the mast!"

Chapter 10

Gordon Littleton became more like his old self every day. The trip to New Providence took only a few days' time, and it seemed as if I'd spent almost every minute of it trying to reawaken the spirit of my loyal navigator. The Gordon I'd known before the Royal Navy arrested him had been a flamboyant and opinionated bloke that frequently challenged my decisions and loved to question my every move. I had always believed (although I'd never admitted it to anyone) that Gordon was a key component to the good fortune and success my crew and I had always enjoyed. It was very difficult to make a rash decision on anything because Gordon was always there to make me think every intricate detail of every mission through until there was almost no room for error. During these trials, as I liked to call them, I frequently made it known to Gordon that I was the captain and if I wanted his bloody input I'd ask for it. When I said the words, I meant them. It was only later, after a successful raid or battle occurred, that I would come to realize many of the points he'd forced me to listen to came to fruition once the action began. It seemed that this was always the case, but I was always too stubborn to give Gordon his due praise. I suppose I feared that if I did so the opinions and input from him would only get worse.

The Gordon Littleton that I rescued from the clutches of Captain Edward Sutton was not the same man that had been taken from me—at least not at first. The new Gordon Littleton was unusually cooperative with everything I asked of him. One would think that this new "attitude" (for lack of a better word) that had taken hold of my good friend would've been something that I would eagerly embrace. To be honest, at first I did. But as time grew on I found myself longing for the old Gordon to return.

When I'd finally had enough of his strange behavior, I did the only thing I knew to do. I told him. His initial response was surprise and an immediate denial of my charges. I suppose it would not have been so bad if it were not so blatantly obvious that Gordon believed and meant the words that he spoke. It was at that moment that I finally decided what needed to be done to awaken my old friend's true spirit. I was going to have to do something so appalling and egregious that Gordon would have no choice but to challenge my authority.

I'd noticed that Gordon had taken quite a liking to Joe, the former slave that joined my crew back in Port Royal. Joe was the epitome of what one would envision to be a gentle giant. Everyone on the crew liked the man, and he was arguably the hardest working seamen that I had. So, with that in mind, I gathered Joe and Andrea into my quarters to tell them of my plan to bring Gordon to his senses. Joe smiled his wide toothy smile as he listened, and Andrea even managed to crack a half-smile. That was a welcomed sight. Andrea had probably been the one member of my crew that I trusted the least.

The truth was I wanted to trust her. I just wasn't sure if I could. She was the daughter of the fearsome Captain Winston Trimble, the very pirate we were hunting. She'd been very adamant about not wasting time and effort on a rescue attempt for Gordon. I was beginning to think she just didn't like the man, but when we managed to rescue him from Captain Sutton, I could see the relief on her face. I suppose it could've been relief that her own skin had survived the battle, but I just wouldn't allow myself to think that way. She had to be happy that Gordon, the very man that risked his own neck to rescue her, had been rescued and was back where he belonged. And now, her willingness to help me try to help Gordon just reinforced that belief.

When I was satisfied that everyone was comfortable with their roles, the three of us went about our respective parts. Joe performed his usual chores that day and when it came time for him to go below the decks to see to our chickens, I waited a few moments, and then asked Gordon if he minded helping Joe gather eggs and hardtack from the store to take to Jolly Jack. As expected, he eagerly obliged and went to help Joe. Meanwhile, Andrea waited in the ship's galley in place of Jolly Jack and I hid in the shadows to watch the entire scene unfold.

When Joe and Gordon arrived with their goods, Andrea wasted no time making a fuss about the lack of eggs that were in Joe's basket.

"This cannot possibly be all of the eggs we have," she snapped.

Joe pulled the kerchief from his head and nervously wrung the cloth in his large hands. "Yes, ma'am, that's all that was there today," he replied, his head toward the floor.

Andrea glanced down at the basket and then back to Joe. "I don't believe you," she argued. "The reason I'm here is because Jack told the captain that he suspects you and your friends are stealing food, Joe. Redd wanted me to look in to the matter."

"Now hold on a minute," Gordon interrupted. "I was with Joe and he got all the eggs that were down there. He can't make the chickens lay them any faster!"

Andrea turned to Gordon and made no attempt to hide the fact she was annoyed with his interference. "Gordon, my dear," she began. "Do you think our suspicions just began today?"

Gordon opened his mouth to speak, but thought better of it.

"I'm afraid we've been dealing with this matter ever since Joe and his friends boarded *Henrietta*," she said. "I know that you've only known Joe for a couple of days, but take it from someone who's been at sea with him while you were away, this man is stealing food. Why do you think that the captain sent you down to help him gather the food?" she asked, raising an eyebrow.

Gordon's eyes widened as he suddenly realized that I'd tricked him into spying on Joe. I saw a brief flash of the old Gordon there, but just as quickly as it had arrived, it then vanished. He took a long look at Joe. The large man was still fumbling with his kerchief and staring at the wooden planks below his feet. "Joe, are you and your friends taking food?"

Joe's head rose quickly and he wasted no time answering. "No sir" was the reply. "We eat our meals with the rest of the crew... that's the truth, Mr. Littleton. I swear it."

Gordon nodded then looked back to Andrea. "I'm sorry but you are wrong. This man is not taking food and I just witnessed him gather all of these bloody eggs. You don't have any hard evidence to back up your accusations."

My time had finally arrived to enter the scene. I stepped forward into the dim light that shone from a nearby lantern. My sudden presence briefly startled Gordon. "But Gordon, you didn't arrive to help him until he'd already been down there for a few minutes, mate," I said softly. "He had time to hide some of the eggs when he heard you approaching and I bet some of his friends have probably already gone and gathered them while you have all been discussing the matter here. I know you've taken a liking to the man... the truth is, we've all taken a liking to him. But the scoundrel and his knaves are bloody scum, they are."

There was no mistaking the utter look of shock all over Gordon's soft face. He literally gasped as if the last sentence I'd spoken had been a slap in the face. It was all I could do not to smile, but I had to wait for Gordon's tirade to begin. I would only be comfortable that he was back when that moment began. He looked to Joe again, an expression of pure pity in his eyes.

"Please, Mr. Littleton," Joe said. "You have to believe me... we didn't take any food, sir."

"I believe you, Joe," Gordon replied, and then he looked back to me. "What will his punishment be?"

"He signed the articles," I said. "You bloody well know what his punishment will be. We must treat him like any other pirate on this ship. We'll drop him off at the next strip of land we see."

"You can't maroon him, Redd," Gordon said in his most pleading tone. "At least not yet. Give me some time to prove his innocence."

I shook my head. "Sorry, mate. I can't do that. I've got no tolerance for thievery." I stepped forward and grabbed Joe's massive forearm. "Let's go, mate. You'll remain in the brig until we spot a piece of sand to drop you on." Joe hung his head low but did not utter a single word in argument.

I turned away and began to lead him away. It was beginning to concern me that Gordon was not putting up much of a fight on the matter... and then it happened. Joe came to an abrupt stop, his free arm now clutched in Gordon's grasp.

"I can't let you do this, Captain," Gordon said. "This man is innocent and I will not stand idly by while you condemn him to death."

I tugged Joe toward me. "I do not need your permission, or your thoughts on the matter," I growled. "As I said before, Joe signed the articles just like everyone else."

Gordon tugged Joe back to him. "You're not taking him, Redd."

I pulled Joe to me again. "Yes, I am. Now get your bloody hands off of him or you'll soon find yourself joining him."

I watched as Gordon's face turned to a shade of red I had not seen since that night at the Parrot's Landing when I told him of my plan to rescue Andrea. His eyes narrowed and his jaw clenched. Then, quick as lightning, he drew Andrea's cutlass from its scabbard before she even knew what was happening. Gordon then pointed the blade toward my throat.

"Let him go," he said coldly. "And draw your steel."

Suddenly it seemed that the old Gordon had returned, and in a sad twist or irony, I quickly found myself longing for the cooperative one again. I carefully let go of Joe's arm and allowed a smile to creep across my face.

"There's the Gordon I know," I said calmly. "Good to have you back, mate."

"Draw your steel!" he exclaimed.

"Now just calm down, you rascal," I replied, raising both of my hands. "I will not draw anything. Put your sword down so we can talk about this."

Gordon kept his icy gaze on me, but directed his voice to Joe. "Go and get Oliver Langley, tell him to get down here quick. Tell him I need his help."

Joe looked over at me, wide-eyed and confused.

"Stay right there, Joe," I told him. "I told you our little plan would work. See how smart your captain is," I said, winking at him.

Joe didn't return a smile; he just continued to stare at Gordon's sword pointed at my throat. I suppose from his point of view, I looked anything but smart at the moment. However, my statement did seem to get Gordon's attention.

"What are you talking about?" he asked.

"This was all a bloody trick, mate," I answered. "I was just trying to get a rise out of you so that the old Gordon would return to us."

Gordon's hard expression softened; and the sword lowered slightly. "You... tricked me?"

I slowly put my palm on the flat side of the cutlass and gently pushed it away. "Aye, you were doped, mate."

"We were just trying to get you back to your old self, you dolt!" Andrea chimed in.

Gordon looked over at Joe. He was still wide-eyed and somehow seemed to be the most uncomfortable person in the room. "Is this true?" Gordon asked him.

The big man nodded slowly in response. "We were just trying to help you, Mr. Littleton."

Gordon dropped the cutlass and took a step back. He then peered over at me with a glare that was all too familiar. "You're lucky I didn't hack your skull asunder," he quipped.

"Aye, I could tell you would have too," I replied. "Must be that killer instinct."

Gordon scoffed at that and trudged back to the waist without saying another word.

When he was gone, Joe asked, "Is that the Gordon you wanted to come back?"

I nodded and smiled.

Joe stared at me in disbelief. "But... he tried to kill you, Captain!"

"Aye, verily... and I wouldn't have it any other way, mate."

Chapter 11

I've never considered myself to be very religious, which I'm sure has a great deal to do with why I'd been so skeptical about the tales Governor Winters had told about King Solomon's ring and the incredible stories of Captain Trimble using it to control the kraken. Having said that, when I think of heaven, only one sort of place comes to mind: New Providence.

During my heavenly daydreams, I dreamt of lying in a hammock on the beach while the damp, fanning breeze that rolled in from the crystal-clear sea kept me cool. The only place on earth I knew of to fit the bill so perfectly was New Providence. It was the ultimate pirate haven and any pirate that wished to retire in paradise almost certainly chose it to live out their final days. It was the site that Andrea's uncle, Morgan Trimble, had chosen.

The water surrounding the island was shallow, so a large ship had to drop anchor a great distance from shore. This inconvenience was part of what made the island such a good hide out for pirates. An English war ship would be unable to sneak up and make a surprise attack.

When *Neptune's Castle* arrived during the morning, Andrea and I took a longboat to shore so that we would have plenty of time to search for Morgan Trimble and question him on the whereabouts of the mysterious chest that Andrea said would be the "bargaining chip" we would need to have a chance against her father. Ricardo La Salle's ship would also be arriving soon, and I left instructions with Gordon and Langley to inform him of our whereabouts and bring him up to speed on our immediate plans. Robert Lynch was also instructed to allow portions of the crew to spend a couple of hours at port in shifts, for it was my hope that we would be ready to set sail again before the sun set.

The town seemed unusually quiet when we arrived, but then I remembered what time of day it was. Most of the pirates were probably hung over and sleeping off their drunkenness from what was undoubtedly a wild night before. When I took the time to look around, there was a great deal of evidence of this as there seemed to be passed out (or dead) pirates sprawled out in every alleyway. Even the docks were strangely quiet. There were way too many fishing boats still docked for that particular time of the morning.

I followed Andrea to a large tavern near the corner of town. I'd been to New Providence many times, but somehow, I'd never had the pleasure of drinking in this particular establishment. A weathered, wooden sign hung over the front door. Chipped blue paint over a white background displayed three scrawled words: The Blue Dolphin. There was even a faded drawing of a blue dolphin under the arched words.

We entered the building and once inside, it seemed that the previous night of hard living had taken its toll on many of the Blue Dolphin's patrons. There were pirates sleeping on top of tables, and some were even lying underneath them. The few that were awake were cradling their sore heads, and I wasn't sure if the soreness they seemed to be experiencing was from a hard night of drinking or fighting. I was not about to ask either.

Despite the gloomy setting, there was still a young fellow in the corner of the room sitting upon a stool. There was a large hat upon his head with what appeared to be a peacock feather protruding from the band. He was strumming on a stringed instrument a melody far too joyous for the current mood in the room, and underneath his thin mustache, there was a toothy smile that seemed just as out of place. No one seemed to be paying him any mind.

Andrea marched straight to the bar and when the bartender noticed her approaching, I saw something in his eyes that I wasn't expecting. He suddenly seemed very nervous. He recognized her and did not seem to be thrilled to see her. The bartender was a short, portly man. He was bald, save the horseshoe band of dark brown hair that wrapped around the sides and back of his head. He, like the musician, had a mustache, but his was much fuller, and it seemed to take the attention off the top of his shiny, bald head. He wore a blue cotton shirt that matched the color of the dolphin on the outdoor sign, and a white apron. Andrea opened her mouth to speak to him, but it was I that spoke first. I took a seat at the bar and promptly ordered a drink.

"Bartender, I'll have a glass of your finest wine, sir," I declared as I slapped a piece of eight down on the counter top.

The bartender quickly filled my request and my golden coin disappeared with a swipe of his hand. He then turned his attention back to Andrea. She in turn was still looking at me, annoyance all over her face. I returned a smirk and then took a pull from the glass in front of me.

"How are you, Willie?" she asked the bartender in a cheerful tone that sounded forced.

"Doing quite well... busy, but well," he replied calmly. "Can I get you a drink, Andrea?"

She shook her head. "No, not here to drink, Willie," she said.

Willie wiped his hands on his apron and then took a seat behind the counter. He then reached underneath the counter and I noticed Andrea's right hand move quickly to her pistol. Willie saw the gesture too, and he swiftly returned his hand to the top of the counter again. In said hand, Willie clutched a green bottle by the neck. Andrea relaxed and watched as he worked the cork out and proceeded to pour himself a drink. Then, with a shaky hand, he put the cup to his lips. After his thirst had been quenched, he wiped his mouth with his sleeve and said, "So how can I help you today, Andrea?"

"I'm looking for my uncle," she replied.

Willie seemed taken aback. "You don't know where he is?"

Andrea smiled sheepishly, but only for a moment. "I haven't been the best niece, Willie," she answered, and then her mood turned serious. "Do you know where he is or not?"

Willie shook his head. "I'm sorry, but I do not. However, I believe that gentleman over there may be able to assist you," he said, pointing to darkened corner of the room.

I could see the figure of a man—an old man—seated in that darkened corner, but it was impossible to make out anything else about him.

"There are no 'gentlemen' to be found in this establishment," Andrea replied. "Who is he?"

"That there is one of the meanest scallywags in all of New Providence," Willie replied. "He's not one to trifle with."

"He's an old man," Andrea said, dismissing any notion that he could be dangerous. "Does he have a name?"

"Aye, I'm sure he does, but all anyone ever calls him is 'the Captain.'"

I squinted my eyes in a futile attempt to get a better look at the mysterious old man. Now my own curiosity was peaked. "So how exactly do you know that this man is dangerous?" I asked, sliding my now empty glass over to Willie.

He reached for the bottle of wine again and looked my way. When I shook my head he returned the bottle under the counter, and then wiped down the counter where my glass had been sitting.

"I'm a bartender, sir," he replied to me. "I don't just pour drinks. I'm a professional listener. I listen when people have no idea that I'm listening. I've heard plenty of stories about the Captain. He's a former pirate captain and one of the meanest there ever was."

"Well if he's a former pirate captain then surely he knows my father," Andrea said.

"Aye, he definitely knows your father," Willie said quickly. "And I strongly suggest you don't tell him that you're Winston's daughter!"

"I don't understand why not," I asked.

"No, he's probably right," Andrea answered. "There aren't many people that are friends with my father."

"No, you're not following me," Willie said. "He has a history with your father. He despises your father. There's a lot of bad blood there." Willie paused a moment in thought. "Come to think of it, it's probably not a good idea for you to go and speak to him at all. I'll find someone else that may know the whereabouts of Morgan."

"No," I said abruptly. "That won't be necessary. I'll go talk to him."

"Thanks, but no thanks," Andrea said. "I can speak for myself."

She turned to walk toward the old man, but I grabbed her by the arm.

"Don't be a bloody fool," I snapped. "Take a seat at the bar and give me five minutes."

Andrea looked down at my hand on her arm, and I saw that familiar flash of anger. I gently released her arm before it got worse. She then turned her attention back to the old man, and then back to me again. "Okay," she agreed. "I suppose it could cause a scene if he discovered who I was."

"Right, and we don't need the attention. Give me five minutes and then we'll be on our way."

She nodded, and then said, "Before we go any further with this I need you to understand that you cannot go with me to confront my uncle."

"Why the devil not?"

"I don't have to give you any reasons, Redd," she replied. "He's my uncle and I prefer to discuss the matter of my father alone with him. However, if you must know, he is not going to tell me where my father's chest is with you there. He does not know you and will not trust you."

"And suppose he doesn't want to give you the whereabouts of the chest. You said yourself that the only other man that knows its location is your uncle. What if you ask him about the chest and he reacts in a way that you do not expect? What if he reacts violently?"

"He is my uncle, you scug," she snapped. "If you're making these assumptions based on the behavior of my father, then you are mistaken."

"Alright, so what will you do if he refuses to tell you where the chest is?" I asked.

"Then I'll persuade him," she replied with an icy stare.

"I don't mean to interrupt," said Willie suddenly. "But the Captain seems to be leaving."

Andrea and I both looked around just in time to see the old man disappear out the door.

"Give me five minutes," I told Andrea as I retreated after him.

I charged into the street outside. It was beginning to get noticeably busier than it was when Andrea and I had first arrived. I spotted the old man moving quickly down the street and then abruptly dart around a corner into an alleyway. I, rather carelessly, jogged after him and once I'd entered the alleyway I soon realized just how careless I'd been. The old man was standing before me with his pistol pointed straight toward my chest. He was tall and dressed in all black. He had a large hat with a wide brim pulled down low on his face. I could just barely make out his eyes in the shadows. The long coat he wore looked expensive and he had a black cape draped across his back.

"Take it easy, mate," I said in a voice just above a whisper. "I mean you no harm; I just wanted to ask you a question."

The old man cackled and there was nothing friendly about his laugh. His eyes narrowed and he took a step forward. "Do you think I'm a fool, Redd? You've come to kill me... that's why you're here. I may be old now but I still have me wits. Did you really think I wouldn't notice you and that pretty blonde lass plotting at the bar? I watched the whole thing. I caught the two of you watching me."

For a moment, I was very confused. The man seemed to know who I was and his erratic behavior and movements suggested that he even feared me... but why? I bit my lip as I concentrated hard on the man's face. The more I looked the more it seemed there was something vaguely familiar about my assailant.

"Old man, have you gone daft?" I asked. "Although you look slightly familiar, I do not know who you are. Tell me your bloody name so that I may make some sense out of this predicament."

The old man moved his head in such a way that I got my first good look at his eyes. They were yellowed from scurvy, but more interesting than that, I could see the bewilderment in them as well. He seemed surprised that I did not recognize him and I assumed he was mulling over even telling me his name. I kept waiting for a moment in which he would lower his weapon, but the moment never came.

"You truly don't know who I am, lad?" he asked.

I shook my head. "I'm sorry, sir, but I do not. Me and the pretty lass you spoke of came into the tavern looking for someone. We asked the bartender and he directed us to you. That's why we were watching you."

"I see," the old man said, and he seemed to relax a bit. However, the pistol remained pointed directly at me. "Well, who are you looking for?"

"A man named Morgan Trimble. He sailed under Captain Kidd and after he escaped the gallows he settled down here."

The old man smiled, and there was no mistaking the relief upon his tired and weathered face. "I see… well, as it chances, I do know where you can find Morgan," he said.

"Good. Tell me where he is and I'll be on my way."

"What do you want with Morgan?"

My jaw clenched as I tried to think of an answer. I wasn't expecting him to question me on why I needed to see Morgan.

"Well, actually I'm not the one that needs to see him. The birdie in the bar has business with him," I said.

The old man cocked his head sideways as he tried to understand. "She's a hussy?"

"No, you numbskull, not that sort of business! Her business with Mr. Trimble is none of your concern. Just tell me where we may find him and I'll be on my way."

"You're mighty bossy, lad," he replied. "Seeing how you're on the other end of my pistol and all, I'd expect you to be a tad more respectful."

I said nothing because if I'd said what I wanted to say, I believed the scoundrel would've gone and put a ball between my eyes. He eyed me for a long moment and when he was satisfied I was not going to say anything else, he said, "Return to the docks and look for a dirt trail that begins behind the blacksmith's shop. Follow that trail until you reach the top of the hill. That's where the homestead of Morgan Trimble will be. Now get out of my sight before I have to waste a perfectly good ball on your rotten carcass."

It was at that moment that Andrea appeared at the entrance to the alleyway. The old man stood his ground and continued to point his weapon at me.

"What's going on here?" Andrea asked, surprised to see a gun pointed at me.

"I have the situation under control," I said calmly.

"It doesn't look like it," she replied. "Did he tell you where to find Morgan?"

"Aye, he did," I answered. I told her what the old man had said.

"Very good." She then looked toward the man in black. "Thank you, kind sir," she said.

With that, the man took off his hat and gave a slight nod. He finally lowered the weapon and began to slink away farther into the alley. As he turned away I suddenly glimpsed something that I had not noticed the entire time I'd been speaking with him… something that had been covered by the very large hat upon his head. He only had one eyebrow.

"Alright, I'm going to go speak to my uncle and I'm going to do it alone, Redd," Andrea stated, fully expecting me to argue with her again. Had I not just experienced a startling revelation, I probably would have argued fiercely to go with her, but fortunately (or perhaps unfortunately) for her I now had something far more important to do at the present time.

"Okay, you go ahead," I said, still watching the man in black walking away. "I'll meet you at the docks when you're done."

Andrea had opened her mouth and no doubt had a retort ready for disposal. When she finally processed what I'd said, she stared at me a moment and then back to the man in black.

"Redd, who is that man?" she asked.

"His name is Charles Higgins," I replied. "He's the man that murdered my father."

Chapter 12

As I chased after my father's murderer, I felt my pulse quicken substantially. I felt as if I'd never ran faster in all my life and as I drew near my target, he turned his head and spotted me. He then took off running, but it was a pointless effort. I easily tackled the man to the ground. His hat flew from his head and I heard his skull collide with the cobblestone when he fell. He lay on his back, undoubtedly woozy from the blow he'd just taken, but he was still conscious enough to reach for his pistol. The gun was lying about a foot away from his hand, and I wasted no time kicking the weapon out of his reach. I then straddled over him and put my blade to his throat. We were still in the alleyway and there was no one within ear shot to help him. His life was completely in my hands now.

"Mr. Higgins, I've waited all my life for this moment," I whispered to him.

The fear in his eyes was very apparent, and it surprised me to see such emotion from the leech that lay before me.

"Redd, my boy," he said, almost gasping. "I knew you'd recognize me... I just knew it."

"I could never forget the eyes of such a vile creature like you," I growled, pressing the blade ever so slightly tighter on his throat.

Higgins grabbed my wrists with both hands and tried to push the blade back, but to no avail. "I always knew this day would eventually come as well," the wretched old man said, and then he began to sob. "I swear to you, boy, if I could take back what I did to your father, I would. I swear it upon my soul!"

"You have no soul!" I snapped through clenched teeth. "You're a monster!"

"Aye," he sobbed. "I am... I am... 'tis true, it is! Please take pity on me, boy!"

As Charles Higgins began to blubber like a baby in front of me, I felt myself feeling an emotion I never would have believed I'd feel in that moment. I felt pity and I hated myself for it. How could I possibly feel pity for a man that had killed my father in such a nightmarish fashion? How I could I feel pity for someone so brutal? As these thoughts washed over me, I felt myself releasing the tension on Higgins's throat.

"Where have you been all this time?" I asked.

"After Captain Bloodbane died, and you left us, the men voted me captain of *Dawn Breaker*," he said, still whimpering. "I had a good run and my men saw me a good captain, Redd. I dare say you'd have seen it so yourself, had you stayed with us."

With that suggestion, I hit him. "How dare you?" I snapped at him. I grabbed the collar of his coat and jerked him closer to my face. "I've heard the story about what happened to *Dawn Breaker*. Captain Trimble tracked the bloody ship down and turned it into splinters. He filleted the crew before he did it. If you were such a good captain, then why are you still alive? You should've died with the rest of those poor souls I knew so well."

Charles Higgins began to sob again and it was becoming hard to even understand what the man was saying. "I'm a coward, Redd," he said. "I jumped ship and left my men to die when I saw that there was no hope in victory. I should've been dead myself… cannon balls turned the timber around me into kindling and before I knew it, I just jumped into the sea. I wrapped my arms around a cider barrel and floated away from the bloody carnage. I prayed, Redd! I prayed that God Himself would see to it that I lived—and if He did, I swore to change my ways. I was picked up by a slave vessel that very afternoon, just before the sun disappeared. I've been a different man ever since—I have Redd, please believe me!"

To my utter dismay, the pity that I felt for Charles Higgins did not waver. I found myself despising the emotion even more, and it seemed the madder I got, the stronger my pity grew. No matter how I felt on the inside, I dared not let Higgins see it.

"You were just pointing a pistol at me, and the bartender told me you have a bad reputation around here. It doesn't seem like you've changed all that much to me," I said.

"I wasn't going to shoot, boy! When I recognized you, I assumed you'd come to kill me. I was only trying to scare you off. I mean you no harm. People in this town know of my history with Captain Trimble. Most men figure that if I could experience his wrath and live to tell about it, then I must be a mean as he is. Truth is, I haven't done a lot to change their minds either; I just enjoy being left alone."

I stared at Higgins for a long moment, trying to decide what to do. The desire to kill the man had long since passed, but there was still anger present. I finally stood up and returned my cutlass to its scabbard. Higgins began to rise, but I quickly put a boot to his throat and forced him back down on the ground.

"Do not get up until I'm long gone. If I ever see you again, I'm fairly certain I won't be as forgiving as I have been today. You deserve to die, but judging by the looks of you, I'm confident that your time is not far away. God evidently did answer your prayers."

"He did! You see it with your own eyes," he rasped.

"Aye, I do," I replied. "Since He answered your prayers, maybe I can get Him to answer mine as well. I think I'll pray for Him to give you the slow painful death that you deserve. I want your dying breath to be as painful as my father's was. I want his face to be the last thing you think of when you die."

Higgins's eyes widened at the suggestion I'd made. I could tell that the words hurt him far worse than the blow to the head he'd taken when he'd fallen. His mouth literally turned into a frown and his eyes began to water up again. His lip quivered and he said nothing.

"I'm going to turn and walk away from you, and you're going to crawl away. I never want to see you again."

With that, I turned away and slowly walked back toward the street. I knew he still had his pistol, but strangely, I had no fear that he would use it. No sooner had I taken my third step, the bloody man began speaking.

"How well do you know that pretty blonde lass?" he asked softly.

I turned to look at him. "What is it to you?" I replied.

"Do you know who she is?" Higgins said; he continued to lie on the ground.

I turned to walk away, but curiosity got the better of me. I spun back around to face him. "What do you mean, do I know who she is? Get to the point."

"That lass be Winston Trimble's girl," he said. "She's not the sort of company I'd expect someone such as you to keep."

"She's nothing like her father," I said.

Higgins laughed at my statement and continued to lie there, staring at the sky. "I know that an old sea snake like me is the last person you want to listen to, boy," he replied. "But that lass is just as dangerous as her father. You should steer clear of her. She may be pretty to look at on the outside, but inside she's uglier than I've ever been."

I took a breath, trying to keep my composure. "I've been sailing with her. She is nothing like her father and she is nothing like you. As far as I'm concerned, you and her father are one and the same."

"You've been warned, mate," Higgins whispered. "You've been warned."

I turned to walk away again and this time I didn't stop.

***

Before I even realized it, I found myself sprinting back toward the docks to find Andrea. Perhaps it was because I felt that if I didn't get away quickly, I would kill Charles Higgins. Somehow, I knew deep down I was going to regret letting the wretched man go, but at the same time I could not see how I'd get a great deal of satisfaction from killing such an old and pathetic man as he. I truly hoped I'd seen the man for the last time in my life.

By the time I reached the docks, the people of New Providence were swarming around in all directions. I took note that all of the smaller fishing vessels I'd noticed when we first arrived were long gone. There was no doubt they would later be returning with their stores full of fresh fish that they would probably sell right there on the docks. Later, the men would again return to the same activities they'd enjoyed the night before.

I stopped for a moment and panned over the scene before me. I scanned the crowd and tried to look beyond the produce stands and carriages in the street for any sign of Andrea. When I didn't see her I returned my gaze to the docks. There was no sign of her there either, but I did catch a glimpse of another familiar face.

Ricardo La Salle was strolling rather proudly down a pier immediately in front of me. He and the *Jane* had apparently arrived shortly after Andrea and I had entered town. He seemed to smile and chat with everyone he met. As I watched him, I soon realized he was asking the citizens if they'd seen a man meeting my description. I rushed to the pier and met Ricardo just as he reached the edge of town.

"Hello señor," he said loudly. He reached out and shook my hand with a firm grip as I led him toward the street. "That new ship of yours is quite fast! I tried to keep pace with you, but my old girl just didn't have it in her."

I had noticed that *Neptune's Castle* was indeed a swift ship. However, I was unaware that Ricardo had been trying so hard to keep pace with her. This was good news to me, for it was most difficult to find a ship that was both large and swift. Usually one trait was sacrificed for the other. I decided it would be best to try and downplay the significance of the speed of my new ship altogether.

"Ricardo, have you gone daft?" I asked him in a serious tone.

He smirked at me, but his expression was complete bewilderment. I could tell that he was unsure if I my words were sarcasm or an intentional insult.

"My friend, have you forgotten that your load is far heavier than mine," I added. "Of course your ship was somewhat slower."

Ricardo thought a moment, and then nodded. And with that the matter was dropped altogether. He quickly changed the subject. "I've got my men unloading my cats here," he said.

"Really? Just where do you plan to put them?" I asked.

"I've got friends everywhere, señor," he answered. "However, I'm afraid that it is going to take some time to get all of the animals unloaded and settled in. I hope that you're not ready to set sail just yet."

I shrugged. "At this point and time, I don't even know when I'm going to set sail, Ricardo. Andrea has gone to question her uncle on the whereabouts of her father and now I'm trying to find her." I thought of the chest and suddenly realized I'd never told Ricardo about it. I contemplated filling him in, but ultimately decided to wait on it. I didn't even know what the contents of the chest would be, so I was unsure of just how significant it was going to be. And besides, if Ricardo was going to need extra time to get his cats unloaded, then I could use that head start to go and retrieve the chest. Andrea seemed to believe that the chest would be near New Providence so getting it should not take long.

"Well do you know where her uncle's home is?" Ricardo asked. "We'll just go get her."

I took my hat off a moment and raked my fingers through my hair. I was already sweating, and the day was turning into a scorcher. I knew that Andrea did not want me to take part in questioning Morgan, but as I stood under the hot sun I grew more and more impatient.

"I think that I know where he lives," I told Ricardo. "Follow me."

We quickly weaved our way through the increasingly busy docks, and I scanned ahead until I caught sight of a shop with a large wooden sign hanging over the door. There was a black anvil painted on the sign and the words "Bobby's Smithing" were carved into the wood and painted white. Just past the smith's shop, there was a narrow trail leading into the trees. As we rounded the corner and prepared to make the trek up the hill, we were met abruptly by Andrea.

I could see that she was surprised to see me and seemed rattled by my presence. "I thought I told you to stay away!" she exclaimed. "My uncle would not trust you and certainly would not have given me what we needed if you had been there."

I saw her clutching a piece of cloth in her hand. The fabric looked old and tattered, but she held it in such a way that I could not tell exactly what it was. I assumed it was a map.

"I'm assuming you got what we came for," I said, glancing at the piece of cloth.

"Yes," she replied. I saw her glance at Ricardo, and I hoped she'd keep the matter regarding the chest quiet. She discreetly tucked the fabric away into her pants pocket and immediately went and embraced Ricardo. "I never got a chance to thank you for your help getting Gordon," she said, clearly to deflect any questions from him about the cloth.

"It was my pleasure, love," he answered, and glanced my direction. "I owed my friend a debt and I was happy to repay it."

"Aye, and you did repay it my friend," I said. "So, there is no reason for you to continue on with this hunt for Captain Trimble. You should go back to Tortuga… I'm sure Jane misses you."

Ricardo released Andrea and then put a firm grip on my shoulder. "You know that I can't return to Jane until I've helped you set things right with Trimble. There'd be hell to pay from her if I left you to this task alone."

"It wouldn't be the first time you left him alone to die," Andrea said, referring to when Ricardo and his crew were forced to leave me to the Royal Navy while they made their escape.

"And there was hell to pay when I got home," Ricardo quipped. "I was not proud of what I had to do that day, but I had my own men to consider."

"There is nothing to explain," I told him, and I glared at Andrea for her insult. "I was there and I know how dire the situation was. There was nothing you could have done, and as we just discussed, you repaid that debt… if there was even any debt to repay to begin with."

"There is no reason to discuss this matter any further," Ricardo said. "I'm going to help you finish this, so let's discuss our next course of action. What's our heading?"

Before Andrea could answer, I cut in quickly. I was still afraid she might discuss the chest. All I wanted to know right now was where we could find Trimble. That was all Ricardo needed to know right now.

"Did your uncle say where we can find your father?" I asked.

She nodded, and her eyes told me that she understood I was trying to keep the matter of the chest secret. "Aye, he says that my father was just here two days ago to pick up a few supplies. My uncle met with him briefly and was told that he was heading to a settlement he owns near Small Hope Bay. I know where it is."

"Small Hope Bay?" Ricardo said, whistling through his teeth. "He's obviously waiting on a Spanish treasure fleet making its way to Florida."

Andrea's eyes widened. "That's right! How did you know that?"

"I'm Spanish, my dear," he replied. "The waters between Andros Island and the southern tip of Florida are frequently patrolled by English pirates looking to take Spanish treasure. What the fools don't realize, however, is that we Spanish are well aware of this and the treasure fleets are heavily guarded through those perilous waters. There was a time when it was an easy haul, but those days are long over. The Spaniards have grown cautious and it would be suicide to try and overtake a treasure fleet so near the coast of Florida."

"Aye, it would be suicide unless you have a secret weapon at your disposal," I added.

"The kraken," Andrea said softly. "The Spaniards won't stand a chance."

"Well, now we've got a heading," I said. "We'll go and rescue the Spaniards, and maybe we'll take a little treasure for our trouble." I smiled at Ricardo.

"Well, it seems the least they could do," he replied, smiling back. "But Redd, I'm curious. Just how do you plan on defeating Trimble and the kraken?"

I turned to walk back toward he docks and put an arm around Ricardo to lead him along with Andrea following. "Leave that to me," I said reassuringly. "You're not the only one that keeps a few tricks up your sleeve."

Chapter 13

Just before sunset, *Neptune's Castle* was once again sailing across the blue waters of the Caribbean Sea. Before leaving, I decided to tell Ricardo to take his time getting his cats settled into wherever he was leaving them in New Providence. I instructed him to plan on meeting up with us at Small Hope Bay on precisely the second morning after we parted. He assured me that he would be there, and although I'd meant what I said when I tried to persuade him to return home to Jane, I was secretly very grateful for his assistance. I anticipated that it was going to take a tremendous amount of effort and planning if there was going to be any chance of taking Trimble down without suffering vast casualties on our side. Any help I could get was going to help significantly.

Once Andrea and I managed to find a moment of privacy in my cabin, she finally revealed what I desperately wanted to know.

"My uncle gave me a map of an island that shows exactly where my father's chest is buried," she said as she unfolded the piece of fabric she'd hidden in her pocket and laid it flat on the table. "I know this island… I've been there before."

"Well, where is it? We need to get Langley to steer us in the right direction," I said.

"Relax," she replied. "We're already heading in the right direction. It's on a tiny scrap of land between here and Small Hope Bay."

I stared at her a moment waiting for more information. I could tell there was something troubling her… something she wasn't telling me.

"Okay, does this island have a name?" I urged.

She took a deep breath. "Yes—Isle of Blood," she muttered.

Now it was my turn to take a deep breath. "Are you sure?" I asked in shock.

"Yes, I swear I didn't know. Please believe that."

The Isle of Blood was well known in the Caribbean as an island inhabited by a vicious tribe of cannibalistic freaks. Some said that it was nothing more than a scary story, and although I'd never been to the island—or even seen it for that matter—I'd heard enough stories about it that I'd believed it to be a real place. The more I thought about it, the more it did seem to be a perfect place to hide something you desperately did not want another person to find. No one wanted to visit a place like the Isle of Blood.

I glanced at the map. The drawing of the island was quite detailed. It seemed that there was a lot of thick jungle in the island's heart, and all of that was surrounded by wide, sandy beaches. I was thankful that Trimble had not gone to the trouble of burying the chest within the jungle, as evidenced by the large 'X' scrawled on the southernmost beach on the map.

"Alright, do you know anything about this island? Have you ever seen it?" I asked her.

"Aye, I've seen it," she replied. "My father showed it to me once before. He was very adamant that it remain a place I steer clear of. I could see definite fear in my father's eyes when he spoke of it—one of the few times I ever saw fear in him."

"Do you know anything else about it?"

She nodded. "Yes, my uncle said that it is not a place to explore at night. He said that if we must visit the island, it must be done in daylight."

"Very well, I think we can manage that," I said, rising from the table. "I'm going to tell Langley now."

As I turned to walk away from the table, Andrea grabbed my hand and stopped me.

"Redd, are you going to tell him the whole truth?"

"I'm going to tell him to head to Isle of Blood; he doesn't need to know anything more."

She frowned at me. "I think that it is past time you let these men know what they are up against. They still do not know about the ring my father has, do they?"

I turned away from her, angry that she even brought the matter up. "I'll tell them when I feel the time is right. I'm still not sure that I even completely believe the stories about the ring and the kraken," I confessed.

Andrea seemed surprised by the statement. "Then why are you even bothering with all of this?" she asked with a scowl.

I stopped at the door to my cabin and glared at her. "That's a question I've began asking myself," I said. "At first I was doing this to get a pardon from the governor. After what I had to do to get Gordon, I think I can kiss that dream goodbye. I can't decide if I'm continuing this little quest because something deep inside me is truly fearful of what could happen when someone like Trimble has that sort of power, or if I'm doing this because I feel I'm obligated to help you set things right with your father. Either way, I'm in way too deep now, and I'm not going to stop until I watch the *Sea Witch* disappear beneath the water with all her wretched crew aboard. And besides, I'm not the only one on this ship that has an agenda here."

Andrea arched an eyebrow. "Oh really? Do tell."

"Wait here," I growled at her, and I stormed out of the cabin. If she wanted the men to know the truth, then I'd give her what she wanted. I returned a short time later with the men I considered to be the leaders and most valuable of my crew. A very drunk Oliver Langley stumbled into the room first, followed by Gordon Littleton, Robert Lynch, Jolly Jack, Joe, and the gentle giant carpenter, Hale Woodrow. All of the men sat around the large table in the center of my cabin. I took a seat at the head of the table, and Andrea was still seated on the other end, right where I'd left her. I noticed she'd put the map away.

"Thank you all for joining me for a few minutes," I began in a serious tone. "There is a matter we need to discuss, and I wanted the men on the crew that I feel are closest to me to meet with me and Andrea."

"What's this about, Captain?" Robert Lynch asked. I could tell that he was genuinely interested in what I had to say.

"I'm glad you spoke up first, Robert, because you're the main one that I wanted to speak," I said.

The young boatswain's eyes widened and he scratched his head. "Me, Captain?" What do you want me to say?"

"I would like for you to tell everyone why you decided to be a pirate almost six years ago," I replied.

Robert shrugged and shifted in his chair. "Well, most of the men at this table know the reason why sir," he said, confused about where I was going with this.

"Yes, yes, I know most of them know your bloody story, Robert," I exclaimed. "But Joe doesn't know your story and more importantly, Andrea does not know your story. So please tell them," I urged. "Andrea needs to hear this. Her father is Captain Winston Trimble."

No sooner had I said those words, darkness seemed to come over Robert Lynch. The young man, whom had seemed innocent and jovial moments before, soon turned angry and foul at the mere mention of the name Trimble. The candle light danced off the sharp features of his face and gave Robert an almost demonic look.

"Why hasn't anyone told me this is Winston Trimble's daughter?" he snapped. "Captain, please tell me we're not joining forces with such vile people. If that be the case I'm afraid I cannot—will not—serve under your flag any longer. That beast killed my father and I joined your crew with the promise that if the opportunity came about to avenge my father's murder, you would see that it happened."

"Relax, Robert," I said calmly. "Andrea is only here because she believes her father to be just as much a bilge rat as you do. You and she both want to see Trimble dead. You can be certain of that." I glanced at Andrea to see her reaction. I dare say she'd turned a lighter shade of white and seemed frightened at how quickly Robert's mood changed.

"What was your father's name?" Andrea asked softly. It almost seemed as if she was in a trance.

"His name was Nicholas Lynch," Robert replied. "Your despicable father attacked his fishing ship and violently murdered him. He didn't even take anything... my father's ship was discovered drifting aimlessly at sea. My father was lying on his side, and he'd used his own blood to scrawl a single word on the deck: Trimble. I was only a boy then, but I vowed to hunt down that man and kill him."

The other men around the table remained deadly quiet and I kept my gaze steady on Andrea as Robert told his story. She remained in her trance-like state and listened intensely. When Robert had finished speaking, she took a deep breath, rested her elbows on the table, and then dropped her head into her palms.

"I was there," she said. "I was there that day… I remember your father."

"What?" Gordon said, stunned. "You were there? You remember Robert's father?"

"Yes," she replied, still resting her face in her palms. "I remember the name Nicholas Lynch… I remember the fishing boat… I remember it all."

I let another long moment of silence pass before I spoke again. I felt that I'd made my point. "Do you understand what I mean now?" I asked Andrea.

"Yes," she answered, and finally raised her head up again. I expected to see tears in her eyes, but they weren't there. She was visibly shaken though. "There have been far too many nightmares left in my father's wake. It seems everyone knows someone he has affected. He must die… and he will."

"Now that all of you have been reminded of the importance of hunting down and killing Captain Winston Trimble, I feel it's time I also share something else. Something I've kept from you." I then glanced at Gordon and Langley. "Something I fear I've kept from all of you."

"Very well," Gordon said. "Let's hear it then."

Oliver Langley leaned forward anxiously.

"Governor Winters chose us to hunt down Trimble for a very specific reason. It seems that Andrea's father has taken possession of a ring that the governor claims has a great deal of power."

"Power?" Hale Woodrow whispered.

"What sort of power, Cap'n?" Langley asked.

I opened my mouth and then hesitated. I was unsure on how they were going to react to what I was about to say. I wondered again if it was even worth trying to explain.

"Are any of you familiar with the signet ring of King Solomon?" I asked.

"Of course," Gordon said. "It's supposedly been guarded by the crown for years, but I've always thought it to be an old wives' tale. I've heard a lot of nonsense about the ring giving its bearer the power to speak to demons and control animals…" He paused a moment. "Wait, are you going to tell us that Captain Trimble now has the signet ring of King Solomon?"

"That's exactly what I'm telling you, mate" I replied.

Gordon began laughing; it was obvious he thought I was a fool for believing such a story. Jolly Jack joined him, and even Langley shook his head in disbelief.

"Look, I do not care if you believe the story or not," I said. "I'm just telling you what the governor told me—and trust me when I tell you that he is very much a believer. He claims that Trimble is using the ring to control the kraken, which in turn makes him unbeatable at sea. I wanted the men in this room to know the full story before we meet up with Trimble."

I noticed Hale Woodrow shudder at the very mention of the kraken. Gordon continued to laugh and dismiss everything I was saying as rubbish.

"What Redd is saying is the truth," Andrea said suddenly. "I've seen the ring. I've also seen what it can do." She glared at Gordon. "This is not a matter to take lightly."

I was completely taken off guard with what Andrea had confessed. It was the first time she'd acknowledged that she knew of the ring's existence. Suddenly, I was just as intrigued as everyone else in the room. Gordon's laughter stopped immediately, and his smug expression was replaced by shock and disbelief.

"And just what have you seen it do?" Robert asked.

"I've seen my father call the kraken from the deepest depths of the sea and command it to destroy an entire ship. I've seen the kraken wrap its long tentacles around a ship's waist and mast and then turn the whole bloody thing into kindling. I've heard men scream horrific howls of terror that I've never heard before, and I've watched the sea around the ship boil red with the blood of its crew. The power my father possesses is very real and very dangerous. The sooner you all accept that fact, the better the odds are that you can actually do something about it."

The gentle giant Hale Woodrow was no longer shuddering… he was full blown shivering. I feared the large man would begin to cry, and I found myself wondering why I'd even invited the simpleton into such an important meeting. The other men sat still and stone-faced. It seemed everyone in the room (including me) believed that the stories of King Solomon's ring were true now.

"So what chance do we have against power like that?" Gordon asked, and now he suddenly sounded angry. "It won't be a fair fight at all if he's got that sort of power!"

"Well, that leads us to our current heading," I replied. "We're going to an island that has an item we can use to bargain with Captain Trimble."

"What sort of item?" Robert asked.

"Frankly, I don't know," I answered with a sigh.

Gordon slapped the table with both hands and then began laughing like a mad man again. "Oh, of course you don't know," he snapped. "Let me guess, she told you about this mysterious item that will give us a chance against her father," he said, pointing at Andrea.

"I'm not lying. It's why we stopped at New Providence," Andrea explained. "I visited my uncle so that I could get this." She retrieved the map and placed it on the table for everyone to see. "This map will show us where to find my father's chest."

"And if we have the chest, Trimble will not destroy the ship that it is on," I added.

"The chest with contents you are unaware of," Gordon quipped. "Don't forget that part."

"You must trust me," Andrea pleaded. "I'm telling the truth. We have to get this chest before we go after my father. It's our only chance!"

"It's bloody madness, that's what it is," he snapped back.

"It's all we've got!" I shouted, pounding a fist into the table.

There was a long silence, and all of the men were looking at me. They seemed somewhat surprised at my demeanor. It wasn't often that I shouted at a member of the crew... even Gordon. I rubbed my face with both hands for a moment, trying to calm myself.

"Look," I said. "I can't do this without you blokes. I need you all."

"Well, I'm not going anywhere, captain," Robert said reassuringly. "Not until Captain Trimble is dead."

The other men began muttering similar allegiances, and even Hale Woodrow managed a nod that indicated to me he was on my side. Gordon, on the other hand, crossed his arms and leaned back in his chair. He seemed to stare at some imaginary point on the wall opposite him in deep thought. Finally, he allowed his chair to fall forward and then immediately looked my direction.

"I've followed you on every other ridiculous cause you've ever embarked upon, why should this be any different? What's our heading?"

"Andrea has learned that the chest we seek is buried on a tiny island between here and Small Hope Bay. We've learned that Small Hope Bay is where we will have the best chance of intercepting Captain Trimble," I said. I was really hoping I could avoid telling them the name of the island. However, I knew it was a futile attempt.

"Well the sooner we find this chest, the better, Cap'n," Langley exclaimed proudly. "So just tell me the name of the island and I'll get this girl in the wind."

"The name of the island…" I said timidly. "It's the Isle of Blood."

Hale Woodrow turned white as soon as I spoke the words. All of the men seemed troubled by the news except for Joe, who I could only assume had never heard of the island.

"Captain, you've heard the stories about that island, right?" Robert asked.

"Yes, of course I have, but I'm not concerned," I scoffed. "The only time to be afraid is during the night. We are going to find the chest during the day. All will be well, trust me."

"Captain, what happens during the night?" Joe asked. His eyes were wide and worried.

"Rumor has it the island is inhabited by a bloodthirsty tribe of cannibals," I said. "It seems that they are not an active lot during the day, and that is what will keep us safe."

Joe nodded, but his eyes remained worried.

"Gentlemen, I don't want the entire crew knowing everything I've just shared with you. We will tell them what they need to know and nothing more. I need their confidence to remain high if we're going to achieve victory. Can I count on you all?"

All the men nodded and muttered agreements. Langley was the first to rise from the table. He grabbed a bottle of rum as he headed out the door and went straight to the helm. It would be a short trip to the Isle of Blood.

Chapter 14

We arrived at the Isle of Blood sometime during the middle of the night. I awakened the next morning and got my first look at the mysterious island when I stepped on deck. I peered through my scope and scanned the entire beach for any signs of life. When none was found, I then began scanning over the thick jungle that seemed to rise up abruptly beyond the tiny beach like a wall. The dense vegetation was impossible to see through. That fact made me somewhat nervous… the island just seemed too quiet. Andrea, Gordon, and Langley all conversed while taking another look at the map. After they all agreed that we were on the correct side of the island, it was time to get the longboat ready.

I decided it would be best if only those of us that had met the previous afternoon in my cabin conducted the search for the chest. The eight of us made landfall during mid-morning. While Joe, Jolly Jack, and Hale pulled the longboat ashore, Andrea immediately jumped into the surf and made her way to the sandy white beach. She then unfolded the map and began walking up the beach. Gordon, Langley, and I followed, each of us with a shovel slung over our shoulders. The three of us said nothing, as it seemed that Andrea knew exactly where she was going. The breeze that rolled off the sea was fierce and nearly constant, and there were a few times I had to hold my hat on my head to keep it from blowing away. Andrea nearly lost the map a time or two as well, but she was careful and held it tightly with both hands. We walked what I estimated to be nearly two hundred paces when she suddenly stopped. Andrea then took her foot and began dragging it through the sand, eventually forming a wide circle. The circle was probably fifteen feet across.

"I believe it's somewhere within this circle," she said, her golden hair blew wildly across her face.

"Alright, how deep do you think we must go?" Gordon asked.

Andrea shrugged. "Sorry, I have no idea. The map says nothing about the depth we should dig and I unfortunately did not think to ask my uncle."

"Well, that's just bloody perfect," I said, dejected. "Well, let's get started then." I shoved the blade of my shovel into the ground right where I stood. As I began digging, I made sure to throw each shovel full of sand outside of the circle Andrea had drawn; however, I had my doubts about whether her circle was entirely accurate.

Moments later, Joe, Hale and Jolly Jack joined us and began digging with shovels of their own. The only one not digging was Andrea, and I was fine with that. Although she was definitely a pirate, she was still a lady and I wouldn't dare think of asking her to dig. I glanced over at her a few times and noticed her watching the jungle intensely. She had not shown a lot of fear or concern when we'd discussed the legends regarding the cannibalistic tribe, but now that we were on the island it seemed to be at the forefront of her mind.

The progress of our digging seemed to go much faster than I expected. Before long each of us had dug seven holes, each one nearing ten feet in depth. This wasn't my first time to dig for treasure, and I was careful to dig myself a slope so that I could get out with ease. I clambered out of the hole and noted that the sun was directly overhead now, bearing down with intense heat. It was already midday and so far there was no sign of any chest. I wiped the sweat from my brow and looked around at the other six holes.

"Alright men, let's take a break… everyone out of the holes!"

All of them climbed from the earth, covered in sand and sweat, exhaustion evident in their slow movements. Jolly Jack was the eldest member of the lot, and the old sea cook immediately collapsed on the ground, breathing heavily. I knelt down over him and poured a stream of cool water from my canteen over his face. This seemed to breathe new life into him and he thanked me. I handed the canteen to the old pirate and he drank his fill. I looked to the others, and they were panting and drinking as well. Langley held the opening of a canvas water bag up over his head and poured water (no doubt laced with rum) into his gaping mouth.

"If we haven't hit anything after digging all this time, I think it's time to move to another spot," I told them as they rested.

"Why are you so sure the chest is in this circle?" Gordon asked Andrea.

She held the map up. "Well, we all agreed that this is the side of the island the map says the chest is on. The text mentions a crop of bamboo near the center of the beach, and I noticed it as soon as we arrived on the island. It then says to walk two hundred paces west and dig fifty paces from the surf. That is precisely where we are digging. Just move to another spot within the circle…it's here, trust me."

"How old is that map?" I asked her.

She looked at the tattered fabric as she thought. "From what I understand, my father made it when he was much younger… it would've been after his encounter with the *Dawn Breaker* that scarred him so badly." She took a deep breath and moved strands of wind-blown hair out of her face. "It has to be at least twenty years old."

"A lot can change in twenty years," Gordon said, which was exactly what I was thinking.

"How do you know that crop of bamboo is the same one your father saw twenty years ago?" I asked. "This beach may be vastly different than it was back then."

"Or it could be almost exactly as it was back then," Andrea replied. "Keep in mind that this is an island people avoid. It's been almost untouched during the past twenty years. I believe that crop of bamboo is exactly the one my father saw. Now, we're wasting valuable daylight. I don't think any of us want to be here after dark. I know that you all are tired, but time is short."

Gordon scowled and then said, "Yes ma'am. I am sorry and it won't happen again. Let me get back to my digging… just please don't whip us."

"That's not funny," Joe snapped, and he looked deadly serious. He wasn't wearing a shirt, and when his large hand tightened around the handle of his shovel, it seemed every muscle in his chest, torso, and arms flexed and bulged in unison.

Gordon turned red from embarrassment, and probably fear too. "I'm sorry, Joe," he stammered. "That was a foolish thing to say, and I apologize."

Joe remained stone-faced for a long moment and then without saying a word he marched straight up to Gordon. The rest of us looked on, unsure of what to do or say. "Mr. Littleton," he growled.

"Yes," Gordon replied meekly.

"You are a very gullible man," he said, and after a brief moment, he began roaring with laughter.

Gordon looked toward me as if he wanted me to give him some sort of explanation. I had none; all I could do was shrug. For a moment, I thought maybe the heat was getting to Joe. The big man just continued to laugh.

"You believe that I'm a thief and you believe I would harm you?" he said, almost crying from laughter.

Suddenly, I remembered the trick Andrea and I had played on Gordon in an attempt to get him to snap back to his old self. We'd gotten Joe to play along too and apparently, the drollery had made an impression on him. I seemed to figure it out about the time Gordon did and the two of us began laughing along with Joe. Hale Woodrow began laughing also, but I think he was doing it because he felt like he should, not because he understood. Andrea, Langley, and Jolly Jack stared at me as if waiting for some sort of explanation, but I just shrugged them off and went back to digging. It was nice to see that Joe was beginning to feel comfortable enough with his new shipmates to joke around, no matter how laughable his attempt at humor was.

***

The digging continued for hours. All of us were exhausted and to make matters worse, Jolly Jack was no longer in any condition to help us. He was now seated on an old piece of driftwood right next to Andrea, too tired to even lift a shovel off the ground. The remaining six of us dug hole after hole until finally it seemed that the entire circle Andrea had drawn in the sand became one giant pit in the beach. All the digging that had been done produced no sign of a chest anywhere. Gordon became more frustrated as the day went on and he began to curse more and more. Langley continued to down his rum-laced water until he was too drunk to even care. His production decreased significantly, but at least he was happy. Joe and Hale, the two biggest and strongest men digging, continued to produce the most. I urged them to take breaks, and on more than one occasion they refused. I knew that they were noticing the same thing that I was noticing: the sun was dropping lower and lower to the west and it would not be long before nightfall approached. The daylight was fading fast. I too was becoming frustrated and I fought it off as long as I possibly could. Finally, I couldn't stay silent any longer.

"There is no chest here," I snapped, throwing my shovel into the sand. "This has been a tremendous waste of time."

"William, I know this will come as a shock to you," Gordon muttered to me, "but I agree with you. If there was a chest buried here, we would have found it by now."

Andrea rose from where she was sitting and walked over to the pit. She peered down into it as if she were expecting to see a corner of the chest jutting out of the earth somewhere that we'd missed. "I don't understand," she said. "This is exactly where the map said it would be."

"Nightfall is fast approaching," Langley said, his voice slurring. "Low tide is coming... we'll have to drag the longboat back a ways to get to the water now."

"He's right," Gordon added. "We should prepare to get off this wretched island before the cannibals come for us."

I looked toward the surf and noticed the tide was indeed lowering. Suddenly, I was struck by an epiphany.

"It's the tide!" I exclaimed.

"What about it?" Andrea asked.

"Your bloody father was far smarter than we give him credit for," I replied. "He waited till the water began to recede before he buried the chest. He knew no one would try digging for it so close to nightfall! The fifty paces from the water was meant to be counted off just before dusk, we should be digging closer to the surf!"

"Aye, the captain is right," Jolly Jack agreed, and he seemed to find a new burst of energy. He jogged toward the edge of the water and then began counting off the paces until he finally stopped a good distance before the pit we'd dug. "Start digging here mates!"

I ran to the spot he was standing and began digging at a furious pace. Gordon ran beside me and grabbed my arm.

"Are you mad?" he asked. "Nightfall is mere minutes away. There's no time!"

"We can do this!" I shouted back at him. "Start digging, we have to hurry!"

Oliver Langley and Robert Lynch began digging on either side of me. Moments later Hale and Joe were shoveling sand out of the way as well. Gordon reluctantly joined in and Andrea and Jolly Jack continued to scan the jungle for any signs of movement. The digging continued for nearly ten minutes when, ironically, Gordon was the first to strike something roughly five feet down.

"I've got something!" he shouted, and the rest of us scurried around him and began digging feverishly.

I looked to the sky and was discouraged when I saw stars beginning to twinkle beyond the dark purple sky. "We've got to hurry!" I exclaimed.

The top of the chest was revealed very quickly and the first thing that surprised me was its size. It was a rather large chest, measuring approximately three feet by four feet. We dug further into the ground and when we reached the bottom of the chest, it appeared to be around three feet in depth as well.

With the realization that our time was terrifyingly short, I commanded Langley and Jolly Jack to ready the longboat. "Get it near the edge of the water directly below us," I said. "The rest of us will meet you with the chest." Both men nodded and scurried away. Langley stumbled a bit but managed to avoid falling.

"Alright men, let's get this chest out of the ground—lively now!"

The lot of us began heaving and tugging mightily at the large metal handles on either end of the chest. It was not nearly as heavy as I suspected it would be, which was a fortunate thing at the current time, but it also indicated to me that the chest's contents did not contain gold (which was not so fortunate). No sooner had we gotten the chest out of the hole and placed it on the beach then a blood-curdling howl rang out from somewhere beyond the dense vegetation where the jungle began.

"What the devil was that?" Gordon whispered.

"That was something bad—something really, really bad," I replied. "Hurry, let's grab the chest and get out of here."

We scrambled forward and had probably made it halfway to the longboat when things began to spiral wildly out of control. The blood-curdling howls grew louder and more plentiful and mere moments later, a glance behind me revealed that a multitude of primitive beings had stormed out of the jungle and were heading straight toward us. It was becoming quite difficult to see as darkness washed over the beach, but I could make out that the beings were naked, and astonishingly, none of them seemed to be carrying any weaponry. They screamed wildly and made inhuman sounds as they approached. Even their movements seemed more animal than human. Although I understood nothing of what they said, I did understand that their incoherent screaming was extremely threatening. There was no way that we would reach the longboat before the wild cannibals reached us. The threatening tone they projected as they approached and the all-around dire circumstances led me to react the only way my instincts would allow. I released my grip on the chest and immediately drew my sword with one hand and my pistol with the other.

"Get that chest to the longboat; I'll be right behind you!" I commanded.

Andrea took the position I'd once held on the large chest, and as she did, Gordon and Robert released the chest and joined my side. The two of them immediately drew their weapons as well.

"What are you doing?" I snapped.

"You can't hold those bloody freaks off by yourself," Gordon replied. "Hale and Joe are strong enough to get the chest to the boat without our help; we'll help you hold them off until it's done. They aren't even holding any weapons; how hard can it be?"

There was no time to argue or discuss the issue any further; the wave of cannibals was upon us. Their vicious assault was met with the cold, cruel steel of our blades. I'd never sliced and hacked my way through so much flesh in all my life. The screams of our attackers were bone-chilling, and I was unable to tell if it was due to the pain they were experiencing or the rage. The continuous showers of blood and flesh did little to slow the barrage of bodies that rained mercilessly upon us.

As I fought the strange cannibals, I noticed that that their eyes were the color of blood. They were doing all they could to sink their teeth into our flesh as they came at us, and I shivered when I noticed how sharp their teeth were. There was nothing human looking about the teeth in the jaws of our bloodthirsty attackers. The closest thing I knew to compare it to was the teeth of a shark. One bite would deal a great deal of damage and pain to the recipient.

"Back up… we've got to get to the boat!" I shouted at Gordon and Robert.

We began walking backward, and as we did I could feel the first hint of fatigue in my arms and shoulders.

"I can't keep this up much longer, Captain!" Robert exclaimed, and there was a lot of concern in his tone. He fired his pistol and put a ball into the forehead of the cannibal in front of him. His target did not even have time to scream… he fell to the ground instantly and those behind him tripped over him. The thunderous sound of the gun seemed to startle our remaining attackers, and for the first time I felt that we'd gotten a moment to catch our collective breaths.

"Run for it!" I shouted. I immediately turned and ran toward the longboat. I did not wait to see if Gordon and Robert were with me; if there was any chance of us making it, we had to run at that precise moment. Any hesitation would probably result in a painful death.

Ahead of me I could see that Andrea, Langley, and Jolly Jack were already in the longboat. Joe and Hale had just placed the chest inside the boat and were frantically trying to get the vessel into deeper water. I now noticed that Robert and Gordon were on either side of me, both of them running at an obviously faster pace than I was. Remembering how the blast of the gun drove the cannibals back, I turned around as I ran and fired a ball into the crowd. My shot drove into the chest of one of them. This time the cannibal wailed in tremendous pain. He fell to his knees and I could see a steady stream of blood pouring from the wound. His counterparts did not seem as fazed by the blast this time and they just ran around their injured mate as if he were a large rock in the sand and nothing more.

"We're almost there!" Gordon shouted.

We were now in the surf and I could see that Joe had pushed the longboat into water that was waist deep. Hale Woodrow was headed back in our direction with a cutlass in each hand.

"Hale, go back to the boat," I commanded him, and then the worst thing that could possibly happen, did. Once we'd reached knee-deep water, Robert stumbled and fell on his hands and knees.

"Get up!" I screamed at him. I turned to assist him and as I reached down to grab his arm, I knew I was too late. Our attackers were on us and I had no time to get up and defend myself. Fortunately, Gordon Littleton was still by my side and he fired his pistol into the center of the wall of naked bodies as they scrambled over us. Although it slowed the attack, it was not going to give us enough time to save ourselves. Still, I jerked Robert from the swirling waters and I was prepared to take a couple of them with me to Davy Jones's locker before we were completely overwhelmed. It was at this dire moment that Hale arrived and begin cutting through the cannibals with both of his blades in a ferocity that I'd never seen in the gentle giant. Heads and limbs fell to the surf and the water turned red all around us. Robert turned to help him, but I pushed him forward.

"Get to the longboat!" I shouted.

He did not argue, and Gordon followed him to the boat as it drifted farther out to sea. I turned to assist Hale, and as I did so I heard the large man release a wail of pain. Both of his harms continued to hack and flail in wide, forceful swaths, but I was still able to catch sight of a nasty wound on his forearm. Just I was about to rejoin the fight, it seemed that the vicious cannibals were finally to the point of retreating.

"Let's go Hale," I said, tugging at his shirt. "Get to the boat... quickly now."

He did as I commanded, and I glanced at the wound on his arm as he cradled it with his good arm. A large chunk of flesh was missing. It had apparently been bitten out and it looked rather nasty.

Before I followed Hale to the longboat I took one last look at the carnage we'd left on the beach. The silver moon above revealed piles of bodies lying on a sandy carpet of red that led all the way to the surf. Between the cannibals that got away and the bodies left on the beach, I estimated we'd been attacked by at least a hundred of them. There was no doubt in my mind we'd managed to slaughter all but a quarter of that number. When I finally reached the boat, I could barely swim anymore and for a moment feared that I would drown. I tried to get a grip on the side, but my hand slipped off. Fortunately, Langley and Gordon were there to fish me out. I lay in the bottom of the boat for a long moment just trying to catch my breath.

"On my God," Andrea said softly. "Redd, are you alright?"

I nodded to her and then looked around. "How is Hale?"

"Not good," I heard Robert mutter from somewhere near the stern behind me. "Hopefully we can get him patched up when we get back on the ship."

I closed my eyes and nodded. I'd seen the wound and I knew it wasn't good at all. I turned a glance back to Andrea and I stared at her with narrowed eyes.

"This had better be worth it," I grumbled, placing a hand on the lid of the chest.

Chapter 15

Now that the crew and I were all safely on board *Neptune's Castle*, and with the horrors of the Isle of Blood behind us, I could finally focus on Trimble's mysterious chest that now rested upon the floor of my cabin. I took time to light extra candles so that the room was well lit; I wanted to get a good look at the item that was apparently so very precious to Captain Trimble. Andrea, Gordon, Joe, and I surrounded the dirty chest and the only thing keeping us from exploring its contents was an old rusty lock. I retrieved one of Hale Woodrow's hammers and immediately took out my frustrations on the old lock, but it stubbornly held together. I angrily tossed the hammer aside and I noticed the other's jump when it banged against the wooden floor. No one said a word, but they could clearly see that I was upset. Robert Lynch suddenly opened the cabin door and stepped inside. There was blood on his hands; he was sweating and visibly shaken.

"How is Hale?" I asked somberly.

Robert sighed and shook his head. He grabbed a rag from his back pocket and then took a pitcher of water that was sitting on a nearby table. He then wet the rag and began cleaning the dried blood off of his arms and hands.

"It doesn't look good," he replied, focusing only on his arms while he spoke. "He's lost a lot of blood... I patched him up the best I could but I'm no doctor. He needs medicine. He's sleeping right now but I have no idea how. He's burning up with fever."

"He has a fever already?" Gordon asked. "His injury occurred less than an hour ago."

"Yes, but there is no mistaking the fever," Robert replied. "You could fry an egg on his forehead right now. It came about very suddenly, but it seems to have stabilized. I've got the men taking shifts watching him."

I took a breath and rubbed my eyes with my hands. I was exhausted, and I was sure the rest of the crew was as well. It was going to be hard enough getting sleep with the anticipation of the impending battle with Trimble looming over us. The news of Hale Woodrow's condition didn't make things any easier.

"There is nothing more that we can do for him now," I said. "His fate is in God's hands now."

There was a long moment of silence and I considered saying more, but truthfully, I just didn't know what else to say. At the moment, I figured the best thing to do was to return my frustrations upon the locked chest. I delivered no less than seven more solid blows upon the rusty shackle when suddenly it broke loose. Everyone gathered around closer as I lifted the lid, and I could literally feel the anticipation in the room building. There was a wooden box within the chest and it fit inside a little too perfectly. It seemed to me that the box was built specifically to fit inside the chest. There was just barely enough room to get my fingers on either side of it and after a gentle tug, I had the box free. It was heavy, and no sooner had I lifted it out of the chest, I immediately set it on the floor. Fortunately, the lid wasn't fastened down, and it lifted with ease. When I first gazed upon the contents, it took my mind a moment to comprehend exactly what I was looking at. It certainly wasn't what I was expecting and I could tell by the expressions on the faces of my shipmates that they felt the same bewilderment—well, except for Langley.

Oliver Langley's lips curved upward into a beaming smile, and his jovial mood must have looked odd in contrast to the swelling emotion of disappointment suddenly very evident in the rest of us.

"This is it?" I asked Andrea. "This is what we're depending on to give us a chance against your father?"

Andrea peered down at the contents of the box, she looked genuinely displeased, and it was obvious to me that she was just as confused as I was.

The box contained four rows of large bottles containing what appeared to be rum. I carefully pulled one of the bottles from the box and worked the cork loose. The heavy odor of the familiar brew filled my nostrils immediately, confirming my suspicions that the dark liquid was indeed rum.

"I'm waiting on someone to explain to me why these bottles are what Hale Woodrow is suffering over at this very moment,"

Gordon snapped bitterly. "You mean to tell us that Captain Trimble loves his rum so much that he would be willing to bury it on an island full of blood-thirsty cannibals and it's so important that he will refrain from blowing us out of the water because he fears it'll be lost at sea?"

He was directing the ridiculous sounding question to me, and I in turn could do nothing but look to Andrea for some sort of answer.

"I don't know," she said, sounding defeated. "My uncle Morgan even recognized its importance… he was very reluctant to share the map with me. There has to be something else about it that we're not seeing."

"Well, let's get on with popping the corks off of all of them then," Langley replied as he retrieved another bottle from the opposite end of the box.

I snatched it away from him and said, "No, we're not touching another bottle. We're going to put it all back and close the chest back up. There has to be some reason why it is vastly important to him, but quite frankly I do not care. If it'll give us a window of opportunity with the bloody scoundrel, then we'll use it."

Gordon shot a cold glare in my direction, a look I'd gotten all too used to seeing from him. Then he stormed out of the cabin, and everyone but Andrea followed.

"I'm having a hard time understanding why my father is so interested in a chest full of rum," Andrea said when everyone had gone. "Maybe there is something in the bottles," she added.

"Yes, there is something in the bottles," I replied. "Rum is in the bottles, and nothing more."

"Well, I assure you that these bottles have some sort of significant worth as far as my father is concerned. It will give us a fighting chance, and that is all you need. Right?"

"Aye," I said, nodding. "I think it's time all of us get some shut eye. We have a big day tomorrow."

Andrea settled into my bed and was asleep in mere minutes. Something about that bothered me. It seemed to me that she'd be a bundle of nerves the night before she confronted her father and, if everything went as planned, saw him die. When I was certain that she'd fallen asleep, I settled into bed beside her, but it was not nearly as easy for me to fall asleep.

After tossing and turning several times, I was suddenly surprised to find that Andrea had awakened again. She looked into my eyes and I knew immediately where her mind had wandered. She grabbed the back of my head and pushed her lips on to my own.

My first thought was to fight off her advance, but it was a futile thought. Andrea, whether I liked it or not, was a very beautiful woman and her beauty was more than my conscience could handle. Before I knew it, she'd slipped out of her breeches and removed her shirt. As I felt her bare breasts press against me, I soon realized that my own clothes had somehow vanished before I'd even realized it had happened. Our lovemaking was brief, but it was full of passion. Neither of us spoke during the entire ordeal, and when it was over, Andrea drifted back off to sleep, her head on my chest. We stayed that way for probably another full hour and unfortunately, I was still unable to join in her slumber.

A whisper from the doorway of my cabin startled me. I recognized the figure standing there to be Oliver Langley.

"Cap'n, come quick," he whispered. "It's Hale."

I couldn't see Langley's face, but I could hear a strange tone of terror emanating from his voice. I feared that Hale Woodrow was probably breathing his final breaths. I quickly pulled my pants back on but didn't waste time on a shirt or boots. I padded out onto the deck and Langley, rather forcefully, pulled me down low in a squatting position.

"What the bloody hell is the matter?" I asked him in a whisper.

"It's Hale, Cap'n," Langley responded, whimpering.

I looked around in both directions, trying to figure out why we were squatting. The moon provided just enough light for me to make out that Langley seemed to be shivering.

"What's wrong with Hale? Has he died?"

Langley shook his head and said, "No, no... he's not dead... he's up and he's on the poop deck right now."

Now I was really confused. Hale Woodrow had been burning up with fever and near death just a few hours earlier. And now he was walking around the ship? I could smell the rum on Langley's breath, but there was always that odor on his breath. Langley had never acted this way before, and at the moment his eyes were full of terror.

"Well, what is he doing on the poop deck?" I asked. I started to rise so that I could try and get a look at him, but Langley fiercely pulled me back down.

"No, Cap'n, you mustn't let him see you… he'll bloody kill you too!" he rasped.

Kill me too? Either Langley had gone completely mad or there was something very wrong on my ship. I stood and when Langley tried to pull me back down, I pushed him away. I went back into my cabin to retrieve my sword. Andrea was still asleep, still naked and beautiful just as I'd left her. When I came back out Langley again tried to plead with me to get down.

"Stay here and calm down, old friend," I said, trying to settle him down. "I'll check on Hale."

I padded down the stairs from the quarterdeck and made my way across the waist of the ship. It seemed that everyone else on the ship was asleep, just as I'd commanded. I heard something rustle behind me, and I spun around, ready to attack with my sword. It was Langley on my heels.

"I told you to stay on the quarterdeck," I whispered through clenched teeth.

"Hale is a giant, Redd. You can't handle him alone," he replied, a little more composed but still terrified. I considered arguing with him but knew it was useless.

We continued toward the poop deck, and as I began to climb the stairs I began to hear the sickening sounds of a wild animal devouring its latest catch—tearing, snorting, dripping. The sounds made the hair stand up on the back of my neck. Against my better judgment, I continued up the stairs. When I reached the top, what I saw would no doubt haunt me for the rest of my life.

There was Hale Woodrow, suddenly much more alive than he'd been the last time I'd seen him. But at the same time, the creature I saw was not Hale Woodrow. Hale—or what used to be him—turned to look at me, his lips bloody, and flesh dangled from his teeth. Lying in a bloody mess below him was what was left of another member of my crew, but now there was no way to make out who the poor lad used to be. Hale's eyes did not look like his own anymore; the blue had vanished and they now looked to be the color of amber. Those eyes looked strangely familiar, and then it hit me. Those eyes looked exactly like the eyes of the cannibals that attacked us on the Isle of Blood. The same cannibals that had bitten and torn flesh from Hale's arm.

"Hale, what the devil is going on?" I asked, and I felt ridiculous when I asked the question.

Hale just stared at me blankly for a moment and then returned to the sickening task he'd been at when I arrived. I looked back at Langley, and he peered back at me, his eyes wide and still full of terror, but at the same time sympathetic too.

"That's not Hale anymore, Cap'n," he whispered. "Whatever's taken hold of him, it needs to be put down."

I nodded at him, agreeing but not wanting to accept it. There had been no gentler soul on the ship than Hale Woodrow. I figured that the cannibals on the Isle of Blood must have been infected with… something. And whatever that something was, it had infected Hale also. The poor man was suffering, and even worse, he'd violently killed a member of my crew. It was certain that he wouldn't stop there. I raised my cutlass and was suddenly very glad that I'd just sharpened the blade. I dropped it with all the force I could muster, and Hale Woodrow's head fell to the deck with a thud. The rest of his body fell limp, and the nightmare he'd become suddenly ended.

Langley placed a firm hand on my shoulder.

"It had to be done, Redd," he said somberly.

The two of us rolled Hale's body off the deck, and then we did the same with the anonymous victim. It wasn't the burial they deserved, but it was a burial at sea nonetheless.

"We have a big day tomorrow, and we need everyone on this ship focused," I told Langley. "They cannot know what happened here tonight. We'll tell them later, but not tomorrow."

"So how do we handle the questions we'll get, Cap'n?"

"We'll tell them that Hale died during the night, and we took it upon ourselves to bury him at sea. There will be some on the crew that will be angered by this decision, but they'll understand when we're able to explain it later."

"What about the other poor bloke?"

"I'll deal with that myself when it becomes known who he was. You just follow my lead."

Langley nodded and then the two of us spent the next half hour cleaning the mess off the poop deck the best way that we could. I later returned to my bed, where Andrea still enjoyed a deep sleep. I envied her for that. When the sun finally rose, I felt far too tired for battle.

Chapter 16

As expected, many members of the crew were disappointed and angry that Langley and I decided to dispose of Hale Woodrow's body during the night. They felt it was disrespectful, and all of the men made their feelings known. Gordon Littleton led the usual charge and I did the best I could to diffuse the situation and turn the men's attention back to the job at hand.

It also quickly became known that another member of the crew was missing. A young lad by the name of William Bonner could not be found anywhere on the ship. After searching for almost an hour I finally, rather somberly, declared to the men that poor William must've fallen overboard at some point during the night. This was not too uncommon of a thing, so getting the men to believe it was not much of a chore.

The most unfortunate thing about this was the fact that it seemed to add to the dismay and discontent of the men. I needed their minds on beating Captain Trimble and his crew, but now it seemed all they could concentrate on was Hale Woodrow and William Bonner. I felt a tremendous amount of guilt for lying to everyone, but at the same time I had to tell myself that it was an act that very well may save their lives. Anything I could do to ease any pain they were feeling for their lost shipmates was something I was obligated to do under the circumstances.

The first moment I saw Andrea was an awkward one. Or, it was awkward for me at least. Andrea, on the other hand, gave me a devilish smile and a pat on the derriere when she strolled past. The previous night's activities had obviously done wonders for her, and I was glad to see at least one member of the crew seemed happy.

When *Neptune's Castle* finally sailed within sight of Small Hope Bay, I peered through my scope and witnessed a rather concerning sight. There were two ships up ahead, both damaged from what appeared to have been a pretty nasty sea battle. There were plumes of smoke rising from one of the ships, and as I strained my eyes to get a better look, I swore that the ship looked like the *Jane*. Two of the ship's three masts appeared to be broken, and they were flailing about in the wind. I guessed that they must've gotten entwined in the rigging from the ship's third mast. It was amazing to see that it was able to withstand the extra weight and strain. I wondered if it could truly be the *Jane*.

Had Ricardo beaten me here?

I turned my attention back to the other ship. It was a truly massive vessel and it was unfamiliar to me. Its sheer size and firepower rivaled that of my own. The ship had damage also, but nothing as significant as what had been inflicted on what I thought to be the *Jane*. Andrea, Gordon, and Langley stood idly by my side waiting for some word regarding what I could see.

"There are two ships ahead... they seem almost dead in the water. One of them looks considerably worse than the other. We've obviously just missed a battle." I brought the scope down from my face and handed it over to Andrea. "I think that one of those ships is Ricardo's. Take a look at the other one and tell me if it looks like the *Sea Witch*."

Andrea peered through the scope and seconds later brought it back down. Her expression told me all I needed to know before her nod confirmed it.

"That's it," she said. "That's my father. I can just barely make out the red jack on the main mast."

With those words, I began shouting instructions to all of the crew. Langley and Gordon helped in the effort, and in less than a minute my men were at their appropriate battle stations. The time had finally arrived, and I couldn't believe my luck. It seemed that Ricardo had already done damage to Trimble's ship, and hopefully he'd killed a portion of the crew too. I was concerned about my friend's well-being, but now was not the time to dwell on it. We were going to take advantage of the vulnerability of the *Sea Witch*, and hopefully put an end to Trimble's reign of terror and any concerns about King Solomon's signet ring, whether they were true or not.

I fully expected to see some sort of movement by Trimble's ship as we approached, and when I didn't I grabbed my scope again to see if there was any movement on the *Sea Witch*'s decks. I could see what remained of her crew, and they seemed to just be content with watching me approach.

How odd, I thought. Something didn't feel right about any of this. It felt as if we were sailing right into a trap. I turned my scope back upon the other ship and what I saw made my heart skip a beat. I pulled the scope away and rubbed at my eyes for a long moment. I knew I was exhausted from lack of sleep and what I'd seen could've easily been construed as a hallucination. I sighed and then took another look through the scope. I saw the same thing again, and now I began to feel panic. What I'd thought were broken masts flailing about in the rigging weren't masts at all. Now it was very apparent that what I was seeing was indeed tentacles.

The kraken!

If I had not seen it with my own eyes, I wouldn't have believed it. The monster seemed to just be holding the ship in place. It's long, grey tentacles rose up every side of the ship and the *Jane* seemed to be resting on the creature's body. Suddenly, it all began to become clear to me. Ricardo, or someone on his crew, had evidently squealed to Trimble about our plans of attacking him. It seemed to me that he was holding the entire ship hostage until we arrived.

"We're almost within range to fire," Robert shouted from the waist.

"Hold your fire until I give the order!" I replied.

I wondered how long it would be before someone was able to make out the kraken, and how the ship would react to it. It didn't take long at all.

"A sea monster is taking that ship!"

That was the first cry I heard from someone on the poop deck. From then on the men became frantic, some of them even leaving their battle stations in hopes they could get a better look near the bow of the ship.

"Back to your stations, you sea dogs! You've got duties to attend to!" I roared the command with all the authority I could muster and it seemed to work. The men snapped out of whatever trance that had taken over their senses and began to wander back to their respective stations. Some of them I had to bark at individually and whatever scowl they directed at me I returned tenfold.

"Whatever sea monster is trying to send Ricardo's ship to Davy Jones's locker will fail to do so on our watch, mates! Ready your guns and prepare to send that beast back to the hell from whence it came!"

The men roared in unison and again readied their guns and cutlasses.

"It's not the creature you need to attack," I heard Andrea say behind me. I turned to face her. "It's the *Sea Witch* you need to hit first. It's my father that is controlling the kraken."

I considered what she said and soon concluded that she was right. It was Captain Trimble that I'd come for and he was in a most vulnerable position. We may never have a chance like this at him again.

"You're right," I said. "But I've got to try to do this in a way to save Ricardo."

"That's very sweet of you, but I don't know that you'll be able to find a way to do that," she replied. That annoyed tone of hers had returned.

"Well, I've got to try," I snapped, and then I directed the crew to train their guns toward the *Sea Witch*.

"No one fire until I give the order!" I reminded them again.

As we drifted even closer to the two ships, I grabbed my scope again and searched for Captain Trimble. I peered at the quarterdeck until I spotted an older fellow with a tattered bicorn hat upon his head. He wore a long dark canvas coat. The majority of his face was heavily scarred and a black eye patch covered his left eye. The evil-looking man had to be him. I handed the scope to Andrea and asked her to confirm my suspicions, which she did. I then ordered Gordon to go and fetch my speaking trumpet from within my cabin. If there was any chance of saving Ricardo, I was going to have to at least try and reason with the man. When we were finally close enough, I took a moment to adjust my hat and I then gave it my best shot.

"Captain Trimble," I shouted into the trumpet. "I see that your ship has damage. Order your beast to release that ship or I will be forced to finish it off. Don't make me sink your vessel."

I watched as a member of Trimble's crew brought him his own speaking trumpet, through which he made his reply.

"Captain Redd, I presume?" he shouted with a raspy, high-pitched voice. "I don't think you fully grasp the severity of your situation, lad. I can have that ship crushed in a matter of seconds, and then I can turn the beastie on you before you are able to sink this ship."

"You're not going to turn that creature on me, Trimble," I replied.

The savage pirate seemed confused, and finally asked, "And just why won't I, captain?"

At that moment I reached behind me and pulled Andrea forward, I put my cutlass to her throat. She squealed in response, obviously taken off guard, which was exactly how I'd planned it.

"What are you doing?" she muttered nervously.

"Trust me," I whispered.

"Is that my daughter?" Trimble asked, surprise in his voice.

"Aye it is," I answered. "She's a pretty lass and although it'd be a shame to hurt her, I won't hesitate in doing so unless you command the beast to release that ship!"

Trimble held the speaking trumpet by his side for a long moment and stared blankly in my direction. Our ship had now drifted close enough that the speaking trumpet wasn't necessary anymore. He seemed confused by what I'd just said, which in turn confused me. Then, after a long pause, he began to laugh.

"Do what you must," he shouted. "But just know that if you do not tell me you're going to surrender by the count of five, I will order that beautiful animal to crush that ship into tiny pieces of kindling. There will be nothing left... now, *one*..."

"He doesn't care about me, I told you that," Andrea said, pulling away from me.

"Two!" Trimble shouted.

"What about the bloody chest full of rum?" Gordon asked.

"Three!"

"There's no time, he'll kill everyone on that ship. You need to surrender now and we'll reveal the chest afterward," Andrea said.

"Four!"

I noticed Trimble raise his right hand and the golden ring that I could only guess to be the ring that once belonged to King Solomon glistened in the morning sunlight. I could literally see the muscles within the kraken's tentacles begin to tense up.

"Alright, I surrender!" I shouted quickly. I then ordered all of my men to drop their weapons.

Captain Trimble slowly lowered his arm and an evil grin formed on his etched and weathered face. For the first time, I could see his face well and I could see the burns and eye patch on the left side of it that Andrea had told me about.

"Good decision, lad," Trimble answered, and then he ordered his men to board our ship. They threw grappling hooks over our rails and pulled the two vessels together. I noticed that Trimble, although he moved quite well for a man his age, still suffered from a slight limp. No doubt a result from all of the injuries he'd sustained from the battle with the *Dawn Breaker* all those years ago. He gingerly climbed over the railings of both ships and stomped his boots onto the waist of *Neptune's Castle* to make his presence known to all. He spat on my ship when he boarded it then marched straight up to me. He pulled a dagger from his belt as he approached, and I suddenly became very concerned.

"Where did you find my daughter?" he asked, speaking as if Andrea could not even hear us.

"I helped her escape the gallows. You don't seem very happy to see her." I said.

"Happy to see her?" he asked in disgust. "Why would I be happy to see that little sea devil?"

I noticed him glance over at his daughter, and I did as well. Andrea stared at the deck, but when she made a quick glance at her father I could tell there was something else going on here. Something I hadn't been told about.

"You should watch out for her, lad," he said pointing his dagger at her. "If she'll try and kill me, her own bloody father, just imagine what she's capable of doing to you when your back is turned."

"Is that why you marooned her then?" I asked.

Trimble shot an evil glare my way. "Aye, it is," he replied. "Partly, anyway."

"Partly?" I asked, confused.

Trimble strolled over to Andrea and grabbed the side of her head with his right hand. "Have you not told your new captain what you did to get marooned, my dear?" he asked her.

Andrea clenched her teeth and said nothing. She refused to even look at her father. When she wouldn't speak he released her and then stomped back over to me.

"She got marooned because of this," he said, holding up one finger... the finger that the signet ring was on. "She wants this bloody thing for herself. She wants it because she's far meaner than I could ever be."

I looked over at Andrea, and she continued to look away.

"She's not the sweet lass she's probably made herself out to be, lad," Trimble continued. "She's my daughter; there's too much wickedness in her blood for her to be anything but evil."

"All I know is that she and I share a common interest, and that interest is seeing you dead." I growled defiantly.

"Aye," he smiled. "But just don't forget that she and I share a common interest as well, and that is we both want to wear this ring."

"Why can't we just go into my cabin and talk this out like men?" I offered, trying desperately to get close to the chest of rum.

Trimble shook his head and smiled his evil grin yet again. "Because I do not negotiate with any one at any time. That's not going to change today either."

At that moment, he raised his arm and whispered a command under his breath. There was nothing I could do but watch in horror as the kraken contracted its tentacles around the *Jane* in a sickening manner that imploded the ship in mere seconds. I heard the wails of the crew, and all I could think of was Ricardo as I watched the scene unfold. It happened so quickly I never even got a glimpse of my friend as the ship disintegrated and sank into the blue waters below. The ocean seemed to boil as the kraken writhed underwater.

I lunged at Captain Trimble but was quickly restrained by one of his men from behind. All my unarmed men were suddenly overtaken by Trimble's men, and I now feared I'd made a grave mistake in trying to negotiate with the mad man. All of us were then bound with rope, our hands tied behind our backs. During this time, I noticed Andrea had disappeared, only to reappear out of my cabin minutes later.

"Father, I believe I have something that may interest you," she said, holding one of the bottles of rum over her head.

I could tell the bottle was from within the chest, but there was something different about it. After staring at it a moment I concluded that it was the label that was different. It had a red border around the edges and the other bottles did not. I cursed myself for not looking at all the bottles before being so quick to dismiss the significance of the chests' contents. There clearly was a great deal of significance with this particular bottle because it was apparent to everyone on the ship that it had gotten Captain Trimble's attention.

"How did you get that, child?" he asked, concern in his voice.

"That doesn't matter," she replied. "What matters is I know what is in this bottle and I know what it can do to you!"

It seemed that Andrea knew exactly what the significance was with the bottles of rum all along but had lied to us about it from the beginning.

"Hand it over, child," Trimble commanded.

"I will hand it over when you give me the ring," she replied.

With the fact that she lied to me aside, it still seemed to me that Andrea was using the bottle of rum as a bargaining chip as we'd planned. However, part of me kept considering what Trimble had said about her wanting the ring for herself. The way she was now trying to orchestrate a trade for the ring made me nervous. I'd wondered all along if I could trust her, and now it seemed I was on the verge of finding out for sure.

"You are in no position to negotiate with me," Trimble shot back. "I think I just showed you that negotiation is not something I'm willing to do. Now——"

Andrea suddenly made a motion, as if she were about to shatter the bottle on the deck. The movement cut Trimble's words off immediately. Whatever was in the bottle meant a great deal to him.

"I'm not negotiating," Andrea said as she stopped short of releasing the bottle. "I'm making a demand. You trade me the ring for the bottle, and we both go our separate ways."

Trimble stared at her blankly for a moment and then stroked the stubble on the right side of his chin. I could tell he was giving some serious thought to what his daughter had said before making his next more. Finally, he said, "My dear, you hang on to that bottle and come join me on my ship. I'm sure we'll find a way to resolve this matter so that we can both get what we want."

"I will do no such thing," she answered.

I could see the anger in Captain Trimble building to the point that he would kill his daughter if given the chance. Just as the feud between father and daughter about reached its breaking point, something unexpected occurred.

"Captain Trimble!" a familiar voice rang out from among my own crew. I recognized the voice and I instantly tensed up. It was the voice of Robert Lynch, and I feared the only thing on his mind right now was avenging the death of his father. I knew that this was not the right time, but telling him that was pointless. All he'd ever wanted was his chance to kill Captain Winston Trimble and now he could see that it was within his grasp.

"Who dares interrupt a squabble between my daughter and me?" Trimble snapped loudly.

"It was me, you filthy bilge rat," Robert spat from within the crowd of men on the waist.

"Step forward and show yourself, lad," Trimble replied. He hurried to the railing and looked down upon the men. He gazed back and forth until Robert finally emerged out of the crowd, his hands tied behind his back like the rest of my crew.

Trimble smiled that evil grin again and urged the boy to come onto the quarterdeck. Robert hurriedly did and he immediately stood toe to toe with the man he'd wanted to kill for years. The two of them were of the same height, but Trimble had a weight advantage on the much younger man.

"You killed my father," Robert spat with fury. "Remove my bonds and fight me like a man so that I may show you the justice you deserve."

Trimble chuckled and returned his dagger to its sheath. He placed both hands on Robert's shoulders and looked him square in the eyes.

"What was your father's name, boy?"

"His name was Nicholas, Nicholas Lynch," he replied. "He was just a merchant captain, and you murdered him for no good reason, just as you murder everyone else. Take these bonds off and give me the chance to avenge his death."

"Nicholas Lynch, you say," Trimble thought aloud. "I'm trying to remember, boy, but it's not coming to mind at the moment. But it doesn't bloody matter."

He spun Robert around backwards and cut his bonds loose with his cutlass.

"Someone give this lad a sword; I have a reputation to keep up here."

A sword was thrown to Robert and my young boatswain immediately went to work on the most feared pirate captain of the seas. When the battle began, I must confess that I swelled with pride as I watched Robert masterfully trade steel with such a skilled swordsman as Trimble. He held his own with the much older and experienced pirate and as the two danced their battle to the death, for a fleeting moment I believed Robert would defeat him. Unfortunately, Robert made the mistake too many others before him made. He made the same mistake that allowed me to defeat Augustus Flynn. Robert's rage took full control and as he grew tired, his swordsmanship grow sloppy. He managed to contact Trimble's left shoulder, and the old pirate began bleeding. What Robert didn't know, or had forgotten, was that Trimble had no feeling on the entire left side of his body. The cut was unnoticed by Trimble, but Robert relaxed for the briefest of moments when he saw that blood. It was then that Trimble lunged forward and pierced his cold steel into Robert's chest.

I screamed what must've been a thousand curses, and I could hear other members of my crew doing the same. All around me I could see that my men were trying to break free from their bonds, to take up their swords and fight this crew of wicked swabs to the death. All of our curses and struggles only made our captors tighten our restraints further and in mere moments we were all forced silent yet again. I watched through tears as Trimble jerked his sword free from Robert, the blade coated in crimson. He then kicked the young man to the ground. The old pirate knelt and spoke to Robert as he died.

"Young man, as we were fighting I must confess I began to remember your father. You should know that he was a blubbering fool when he died, and what's worse is that the coward didn't die by my hand as you've been apparently misled to believe. He died at the hand of a woman."

I felt my heart begin to race as I feared I knew what Trimble was about to say. I could see the confusion, pain, and disgust all over Robert's face.

"She's the one that killed your bloody father as he begged for his life," Trimble said, pointing to Andrea. "She's just as cold blooded as I am, you blithering fool, if not more so. Do you all truly believe she cares about you?"

I glared over at Andrea and she was already looking at me. Her face had turned white.

"It's not true," she whispered.

Chapter 17

Once again, I was torn on whether or not I could trust Andrea. Captain Trimble could've been playing some sort of sick mind game with me and my crew. But then again, Andrea lied about what she knew about the chest full of rum. My thoughts didn't dwell on Andrea for very long as I tearfully watched Robert draw his last breath and die. He continued to clutch his cutlass so tightly that Trimble's men didn't even bother removing it before they rolled him over the side.

"Get the plank ready," Trimble commanded.

His men did as they were told and I watched as the old pirate marched in my direction. He grabbed the bonds around my wrists and led me toward the plank. I took a step and then glanced back at him just in time to see him draw his sword.

"You know what to do. Let's get on with it," he barked.

I took a few more steps forward and considered the sea below me. The water directly below was already pink from Robert's wound and I knew it would not be long before the water was teeming with sharks.

"You have the power to stop this, my dear," Trimble called out to Andrea. "Give me the bottle of rum and I'll reconsider killing you and your friend right now."

I knew in my heart it was a lie. He had not done a single thing since I'd met him to indicate he had a shred of mercy in him. I wanted to scream to Andrea to refuse his offer. If I knew the man was lying, surely she did as well.

"You're lying," she said. "I'll give you this bottle and then you'll kill me."

"Aye, I could be lying," he replied. "But maybe I'm not. If you don't give me that bottle, you'll never know." He jabbed the tip of his sword in my back and now the toes of my boots were hanging over the edge of the plank.

"Okay, Father, take it," she shouted. "But please do not kill anyone else."

He held out his hand. "Bring me the bottle."

Andrea stepped forward and immediately handed over the bottle.

"Very good dear," he said as he clutched it tightly. Then he pushed his sword deeper into my back. As I felt the blade pierce into my shoulder, I no longer had a choice in the matter. I had to jump.

I managed to plunge into the ocean feet first. I used every shred of energy in me to swim back to the surface for a gulp of air. I looked up at the ship towering over me and did not know if I should be pleased or dismayed that no one was looking down at me. I suppose my situation looked pretty dire and there was no reason to pay me any more attention. I could see that the water was quite red all around me, and I knew now that the wound in my back was bleeding pretty heavily.

The thought of the sharks that were undoubtedly on the way sent a shiver down my spine. It was extremely difficult to tread water with my hands tied behind my back and I knew in a few more minutes I was going to drown. By then it wouldn't matter if the sharks made a bloody meal out of me. I'd never know it. I desperately tried to think of a solution to my problem and just as I was about to give up, a possible solution popped into my head. I could see land all around me. Maybe, just maybe, the water would be shallow enough.

I took in a large gulp of air and immediately began swimming toward the sandy bottom. The water began to get noticeably colder and the light from above grew dimmer the deeper I went. My ears began to hurt, but I kept swimming downward as hard as I could. I finally caught sight of the sandy bottom and fortunately there was just enough light down there to be able to see. I looked in my general vicinity for the body of Robert Lynch. After scanning the area around me for a moment I finally spotted him, his cutlass still clutched tightly in his hand. I swam over to him and immediately backed my bonds to the sharp blade of his sword. After a moment of sliding my wrists up and down I felt the rope loosen and finally break free.

With my lungs almost out of air I began swimming upward as fast as I could. My chest ached and my lungs begged me to take a sweet gulp of fresh air. I clenched my teeth and kept ascending as quickly as possible. I began to feel as if I were going to pass out and shortly after that, I welcomed the idea of passing out. It would've been better than drowning. It seemed that the world around me began to darken again instead of get brighter as I approached the surface. I briefly feared that I was sinking again, but then I realized I was on the verge of passing out.

Just as my lungs felt as if they were going to explode out of my chest, I broke through the surface of the ocean. It was a painful feeling, but I sucked in the largest gulp of air I'd ever inhaled in my life. It took a moment but I finally began to get my breath back and feel normal again. Actually, I felt anything but normal. I'd never felt so alive in all my life.

Unfortunately, the feeling was short lived. I spotted something dark out of the corner of my eye lumbering just below the surface of the water. Then I saw the terrifying dorsal fin of the shark as it swirled around me in circles. The shark must have swum around me at least five times before it decided to try and take a bite. It lunged at me, but the beast had given me plenty of time to prepare. I had pulled my dagger from my belt and wasted no time burying the weapon all the way to the hilt in to the top of the animal's head. There was very little blood, but it was effective enough. The shark thrashed for a brief moment before slowly turning upside down. It was dead, and once again I'd cheated death. I shuddered when I wondered just how many more times I was going to accomplish that feat.

I swam around to the side of the ship where the anchor was dropped. As tired as I was, I was so eager to get out of the water that climbing the rope was a surprisingly easy chore. When I reached the railing I carefully peeked onto the poop deck for any signs of Trimble's men. There were none there and as I glanced at the other two decks, it seemed that Trimble and his men had already left the ship. I could see most of my men lying on the waist, and still struggling to get free of their bonds. I peered over to the other side of the ship and could see that the *Sea Witch* was already beginning to pull away. I crawled closer for a better look, still trying desperately to stay hidden. There were several oars protruding from either side of the ship and it was obvious that

Trimble was trying to make a fast escape. I suddenly had a bad feeling.

I rushed down the stairs off the poop deck and found Jolly Jack Porter struggling to get free. When he saw me he looked as if he'd seen a ghost.

"Cap'n!" he shouted, immediately drawing the rest of the crew's attention.

All of the men began to shout and rejoice at the sight of me. I knelt down to free Jack.

"No, Cap'n, there's no bloody time!"

"What are you talking about?" I asked, and it was at that moment I saw what Jolly Jack was referring to. A lit lantern was dangling from a rope off the poop deck railing. Underneath the lantern, a long line of black gun powder began and continued down the stairs below deck, no doubt ending where our armory, shot locker, and of course gun powder storage was found. The rope that held the lit lantern had been soaked in oil and was on fire. It was an ingenious and cruel design to allow Trimble time to escape the blast.

As soon as I'd pieced together what was going on, the rope burned in two and the burning lantern shattered on top of the line of powder. It immediately ignited and began burning rapidly toward the stairs below deck. I sprang after it, and in my haste, I tripped. I scrambled back to my feet just in time to see the flame disappear down the stairs. I chased after it and finally caught up to it below deck. I quickly rubbed my foot through the powder line creating a gap at which point the fire extinguished. As I breathed a sigh of relief, I looked toward the armory and was shocked to see Andrea buried up to her neck in an open barrel of gun powder. She was sitting exactly where the line of powder ended. She was crying and her blonde locks dangled wildly in front of her face.

"You should've let me die," she said through the sobs.

"If it weren't for my ship and crew I probably would have," I growled at her. "I'm beginning to think that you haven't been completely honest with me."

She shook her head. "It's true, I haven't been totally honest. I'm not the person I used to be, you have to believe that."

"I want the truth about Robert's father. Was the person you used to be the same person that killed him?"

She looked away from me and the tears began to flow again. "Yes," she said softly. "Yes, I killed him. I've killed lots and lots of men. I did what I had to do to survive and get along with my father. But I'm telling you I'm a changed woman. I'm not like that anymore!"

"I'm sorry, but I don't think I believe you." I helped her get out of the barrel and then led her immediately to the brig. She continued to beg and plead with me to believe her all the way. She even tried to remind me or our interlude from the night before in a pathetic attempt to sway me. It didn't work. I was just about to leave her behind and start freeing my crew when she finally did say something that got my attention.

"I gave my father the wrong bottle of rum," she said. "I mean, the bottle is right, but the contents aren't. I switched two of the bottles around. He doesn't have the right one."

"You better speak real bloody fast, honey. Because Trimble has probably just now realized that this ship hasn't exploded. He's going to come back and this time he's probably going to unleash the kraken on us. Tell me what is so significant about those bottles of rum. Why are they so important to him?"

"Because one of them contains an eye," she said matter-of-factly.

"An eye?" I asked with a raised eyebrow.

"Well, actually it's one of *his* eyes. The eye he lost... the reason he wears the eye patch."

"Okay," I said. "So, what's so special about his eye?"

Andrea paused a moment, apparently considering how to explain the rest to me.

"Have you ever heard of a soul jar?"

"No, I've never heard of a soul jar," I replied. "Enlighten me."

"My father should've died after the encounter with the *Dawn Breaker* all those years ago. His body... you've seen how scarred it is. No one should've been able to survive what he went through. The story, at least the way I've heard it, is that my father was near death in a French hospital on the coast of Louisiana. The hospital had a lot of slave help and one of the slaves was a voodoo witch.

She took a liking to my father and told him she knew a way to save his life, but that ultimately it had to be his decision.

"My father wanted nothing more but to get his revenge on the crew of the *Dawn Breaker*, so he agreed to let her save him with black magic. His body was too damaged to sustain his life—or his soul, if you will—so the witch told him he'd have to store it elsewhere. But since a person's soul can never fully leave their body until they are dead, she had to take part of his body to store it in."

"His eye," I said, thinking aloud.

"Yes, his left eye had been burned too badly for him be able to use it anymore. So she used her spell to remove his soul using the removal of his eye as the avenue to accomplish it. His eye is his soul jar. The eye was placed in a bottle of rum. My father soon recovered, and he put the bottle of rum inside of a chest with many more just like it. He made sure to make all of the bottles look the same, with the exception of one subtle difference on the label of the one that contained the eye. Then he buried it on the Isle of Blood. He never dreamed anyone would be able to get it, but he knew if anyone ever did, they could kill him by simply destroying the eye."

"Why haven't you told me any of this before now?" I demanded to know.

"Because I wanted to be the one to do it. I wanted to be the one to kill him. I could've done it at any time, but I wanted to do it and watch him die," she said coldly.

"I suppose you could be telling the truth," I said. "Or you could've been trying to do exactly what your father accused you of... trying to get the ring for yourself."

Andrea didn't argue with me. She just turned away and sat down, her back against the wall of her cell. "I tore a corner off the label that now contains the eye," she said. "And you're right, he's going to come back, but it's not going to be because he didn't see or hear this ship explode. It'll be when he realizes the bottle he took doesn't have the soul jar in it."

Chapter 18

Upon my return to the waist, I immediately began freeing my crew. Once a few of the men were cut free to help me in the effort, things progressed much faster. I knew the men were shaken and disturbed by what they'd seen the kraken do to Ricardo's ship minutes before, but I couldn't allow them time to dwell on it. Trimble's ship was already making a wide turn and probably getting in position for a broadside attack. I ordered the men to hoist the anchor and get into their battle stations at once. Not one man hesitated at the command. Well, except for Gordon, who immediately questioned my strategy.

"He'll turn the kraken loose on us; there's no time to take that ship down," he said anxiously. "We should sail into shallower water. That way the beast can't get to us."

"He's not going to turn the kraken on us," I replied. "We've got something on board that he wants. He's not going to risk sinking this ship until he has it."

"And what might that be?" he asked. "Another bottle of rum?"

"Aye," I replied. "Andrea gave him the wrong one. He's figured it out and now he's coming for the right one. Gordon, I really don't have time to explain. What I need now is for you to take up Robert's position and get those men and the guns ready. Wait for my command."

Gordon sighed and I could only imagine how ridiculous what I was telling him sounded. I hoped against hope that for once in his life he'd trust me and do what I asked without any more bloody questions. He stared at me a long moment before answering.

"Alright then." He headed below deck toward the gun ports.

The *Sea Witch* was too badly damaged to rely on the wind for power. The oars were all she had to get in position. I was counting on the extra man power Trimble had to use for rowing to my advantage. The men would be tired when they reached us and they wouldn't be nearly as fresh on the guns as my men would be. In addition to that, Trimble's ship already had damage to the hull from the earlier battle with Ricardo. If everything went as I had calculated, the battle would be short and the odds would be greatly in my favor.

"Guns ready, captain!" Gordon called from below deck.

"Aye, await my order!" I shouted back.

The *Sea Witch* had finally gotten into position. The ship drifted toward us swiftly, and I watched as Trimble's men pulled the oars back into the ship. Moments later, the black tips of their guns poked through the port holes. They were obviously a well-trained lot, but I was certain they must be tired. I also noticed that Trimble had made sure his attack would come from the starboard side of his ship. There was almost no damage on that side, which told me he'd used the port side to battle Ricardo. Our own guns were in position to fire from our port side.

I wanted to make sure that we fired first, but to do so would require the most precise timing. Both ships were now meeting at the bows and the anxiety I was feeling was unlike any I'd ever felt before. Just before the ships were dead even alongside each other, I gave the order.

"Fire!"

The thunderous boom of cannon fire shook the deck beneath my feet and less than a second later the *Sea Witch* returned fire. I had been standing on the stairs that led up to the quarterdeck, but part of them collapsed almost immediately below my feet. I tumbled onto the waist of the ship and quickly regained my footing. The men around me manned the swivel guns and miraculously none of them appeared to be wounded. The *Sea Witch* had been drifting so swiftly, there was no time for another broadside attack. I immediately ordered the men on the swivel guns to return fire. Their cannons were much smaller than the cannons below deck; reloading them did not take a great deal of time. They took aim and returned fire. I was pleased to see that every shot contacted the stern of the *Sea Witch*.

"Gordon, damage report!" I shouted down the stairs.

"Most of the damage is minor, although there's a pretty large hole near the stern… looks to be above the water line though. I've got two men dead down here, Redd. Several more are injured!"

"Aye, how are the guns?" I asked.

"All of the guns are still operational, but the two men I lost were manning one. We could use some help down here."

I looked around the deck to survey the damage around me. There were quite a few men injured and bleeding. Langley was one of them, but he was still on his feet, his bleeding hands on the helm. I ordered the able-bodied men to man the canvas and get the ship in position for another broadside attack as soon as possible. I saw Joe wandering around the deck doing what he could to tend to the wounded.

"Joe, let someone else tend to those men. Gordon needs you on a gun below deck."

Joe's eyes widened and he seemed surprised that I picked him for such an important job. "Aye, Captain," he replied. "I'll do my best."

"I know you will," I replied. "When we make our next pass, be prepared for battle. I want to board them this time."

He nodded and immediately marched below deck. I then made my way to the poop deck to try and get an idea of what Trimble's next move would be. I was surprised to see that there were no oars protruding from the side. Since the ship was unable to sail, it was now virtually dead in the water.

"They're plotting something," Jolly Jack Porter said.

"I don't know," I said. "We inflicted quite a bit of damage. I don't even think they could get all of their guns to return fire. We probably killed many of the men they had below deck. There may not be enough men to row anymore."

Neptune's Castle caught up quickly and I was unable to see any sign of life on the decks of the *Sea Witch*. There were plenty of bodies, but they were all dead. There were no signs of life below decks either. I couldn't detect any movement at all on the guns.

"We're almost in position again, Redd," Gordon called out. "What do we do?"

"Unload the guns into her hull again," I answered. "I'm not taking any chances."

Again, the thunderous blasts of cannon fire erupted from below deck. Trimble's ship took every shot without returning a single shot.

"Drop the anchor and prepare to board the ship," I ordered.

Once the ships were roped together, I was the first to set foot on the deck of the *Sea Witch*. All my men, save the injured and dead, were right behind me. All of us were armed to the teeth and ready for anything.

"Keep an eye on those stairs leading below deck, mates," I said as I made my way to the door of Trimble's cabin.

I kicked the door open and pointed my pistol in all directions, waiting for the old pirate to spring out of some darkened corner. I grimaced at the ugly sight of what had to be at least fifty human skulls displayed on shelves as if they were trophies. Alas, Trimble was nowhere to be found.

"Captain! Come quick!" Gordon yelled from the waist railing of the ship.

When I emerged from the cabin I noticed most of my men were looking over the side at something off the port side of the ship. I made my way to the railing and my heart sank when I saw what had gotten their attention. About a hundred yards in front of the ship, I spotted a longboat. Captain Trimble stood at the bow of the boat waving, and he was surrounded by several of his surviving crew. Trimble had apparently used his ailing ship to hide his escape.

"What a clever devil," I thought aloud.

"Why can't we just blow him out of the water, Cap'n?" Jolly Jack asked.

"A target that small and that far out would be difficult to hit, especially since he's directly ahead of us," Langley answered.

"Gentlemen, I'd wager that I could hit him with the swivel gun... I'm a good shot. But it wouldn't do any good if we did; you can't kill him that way. He has a soul jar," I said.

All of the men slowly turned and looked my direction in unison. They looked at me as if I had two heads.

"Long story," I said with a grin.

"Someone's cut the lines free! We're drifting away from our ship!" I heard a panicked sailor shout out.

I turned to see for myself and sure enough, *Neptune's Castle* began to slowly drift away from us. The ropes had been cut while we were distracted. I scanned the deck of the *Sea Witch*. I knew we'd looked the deck over for survivors and found none. So how could—it was then that I spotted the culprit.

Andrea, with a hatchet in her right hand, gazed coldly at me from the deck of my own ship.

"You should've checked on me before you left the ship!" she shouted. "After everything that's happened between me and my father, isn't it ironic that the cannon fire from his ship is what blew the door off my cell and ultimately freed me? Maybe our relationship isn't doomed after all. Unfortunately, it seems that yours and mine is. It's a shame... we could've been great together!"

I cursed under my breath and clenched my fist. Somehow, I knew all along that Andrea would cross me. I just couldn't allow myself to accept it. Suddenly the sea below our ship began to boil and bubble angrily. I knew what was coming and unfortunately so did the rest of my crew. I turned and looked back toward Captain Trimble. He was still standing in the longboat; his arms stretched high above his head. That bloody ring shined brightly in the noon sunlight as if it were taunting me. Now that my ship, along with his soul jar, was drifting away from me, he was free to unleash the kraken on us. I couldn't believe the horrible turn things had taken.

My men began to panic as the slimy, gray tentacles of the kraken began to slither up the sides of the ship. One of the tentacles whipped around quickly and snatched up an unsuspecting sailor. The poor bloke barely had time to scream before he was crushed to death.

"Stay clear of those tentacles!" I shouted.

I kept my sword in my hand although I knew it was useless. The animal's tentacles were much too thick for me to cut through. We were doomed, and just as I began to hear the ship's timbers creak and wail their sad death moan, I spotted a slim chance to cheat death one more time.

It was Andrea. She was running toward the bow of *Neptune's Castle* and screaming wildly at her father.

"Father! Please come back for me! I have it, I have it!"

It was what she held in her hand that got my attention. It was a bottle of rum—no doubt the bottle that contained her father's soul jar. I wasn't happy about what I was about to attempt, but it was unfortunately necessary if my men and I had any chance of surviving. I made my way to the swivel gun near the bow of the *Sea Witch* and spun it in the direction of Andrea. The ship had drifted far enough to escape the danger of the kraken, but it hadn't drifted anywhere close to escaping the range of a well-placed cannon shot.

The gun was ready to fire and I carefully grabbed the lanyard that connected to the friction primer. Although I could literally feel the ship beginning to break apart beneath me, I forced myself to take a moment and aim the breech sight to make sure my shot had a good chance. Andrea stood in one spot as she continued to yell and wave at her father. She clutched the bottle near her chest, obviously taking great care not to drop it. I'd cheated death so much over the past few days; surely I hadn't gotten this far for it to all end now. I yanked the friction primer and the gun fired its deafening roar.

Andrea had just enough time to turn and look in my direction. I was glad she had a moment to see that I was the one who killed her. The shot ripped through her body like a hot knife through butter, no doubt destroying the bottle she clutched so tightly on the way. I believed in my heart that she'd been lying to me all along. She hadn't changed. She was just as evil as her father, and she had been using me to try and get her hands on the ring. I had never been so sure of anything in my life, but I still hated that it had come to this.

The *Sea Witch* was literally falling apart now, but I managed to catch a glimpse of Captain Trimble's longboat as I was falling with the ship. He was no longer standing with his arm stretched above his head. He'd apparently fallen overboard, and his men were struggling to find him. There was no doubt in mind that he was dead, but it was my sincere hope that he sank quickly to the bottom of the sea with that dreadful ring still on his dead finger. If it were up to me, it would never see the light of day again.

Suddenly, I was in the water for the second time that day. I looked around wildly in all directions for any sign of the kraken but it seemed to have left the area just as quickly as it had appeared. It was as simple as that. I don't think attacking ships was something that came natural to the creature. It was being forced to do so against its will, and when the power holding it there ceased, the animal fled.

Gordon swam over to me and said, "I think I've had my fill of the pirate life."

I laughed at him and then the two of us grabbed onto a large piece of debris and began paddling toward *Neptune's Castle*.

"Do you think we'll catch it?" he asked me as we kicked.

"Well if we don't, we'll die," I answered matter-of-factly.

With that, he began to kick harder. We somehow *did* manage to catch up to our ship, and we weren't the only ones. Langley had already made it there, and Joe made it soon after. When enough men made it to the ship, we got her drifting toward the wreckage of the *Sea Witch* and picked up any other survivors that we could find. When it was all over, I lost nine men to the kraken. We contemplated picking up the survivors of Trimble's crew from the longboat, but I decided to let fate have its way with them. Cruel and vile men such as those deserved no mercy at all.

I informed the crew that our heading would be New Providence. There would be no returning to Port Royal. Although we'd accomplished what Governor Winters had asked, it wouldn't matter now. He would most certainly hunt us relentlessly after learning that we stole one of the Royal Navy's ships. And the fact that I'd killed his nephew probably didn't help matters either.

On our way to New Providence we came across another piece of ship wreckage floating aimlessly in the ocean. Imagine my surprise when I discovered that it was from Ricardo's ship. There were two survivors on the wreckage, and it was even more surprising when one of the men turned out to be Ricardo himself. Unfortunately, his battered body was in a grave state when I found him. There was a large puncture wound in his left flank, and his breathing was very ragged. His company, on the other hand, appeared to be in good condition.

"Ricardo, you hold on just a little longer and we'll be back in New Providence. Someone there will be able to help you," I tried to reassure him, although I was probably trying to reassure myself as well.

"Señor, you and I both know that there is no chance," he said, gasping for air. "You tell Jane that I love her... and," he tried desperately to get his breath, "you take care of her for me... she's always loved you too."

"She loves you more, mate," I told him. "She'd much rather see you again. Don't make me have to give her bad news."

Blood trickled from the corner of his mouth and I quickly wiped it away. "I'm glad I held on long enough to see you one more time, señor," Ricardo said. Suddenly, his eye's widened as if he'd just thought of something important. He coughed loudly, and tried to sit up. I pushed him back down.

"Andrea..." he mumbled.

"What about her?" I asked.

"She... she..." He began to drift away.

"She what?" I asked him, and I shook him lightly.

He opened his eyes again and looked into mine. "She killed her uncle, Redd... I found out after you left... She's a killer."

He began coughing again and this time there was no bringing him back. The warning about Andrea was the last thing he ever said to me. I felt the tears well up in my eyes and a knot formed in my stomach. I wanted to hit something. I wanted to scream. I'd lost so many close friends over the past few days. The pain I felt inside was maddening.

I then looked around to my other shipmates... the survivors. I could see the pain in their eyes as well, and it was at that moment I knew that seeing me grieve wasn't the best thing for them right now. I was their captain, and it was my job to see to their well-being first.

I glanced over at the only survivor from Ricardo's ship. The young man had tears streaming down his face, and I then realized that my loss was not nearly as great as his. He'd just lost every man on his ship.

"What's your name, mate?" I asked him, hoping he spoke English.

"Macuya," he replied, his accent thick and heavy.

I put a firm hand on his shoulder to comfort him. "Well, Macuya, I'd be honored if you joined my crew. Although our losses are not as bad as yours, we've still lost a lot of men. We could use another good sailor. I know any man that sailed for

Ricardo was indeed a good sailor. He didn't settle for anything less."

Macuya looked down at Ricardo for a long moment and then began to wipe the tears from his eyes. Finally, he looked up at me.

"He wanted me to survive so that I could tell you to take care of Jane. He said he wanted you to look after his cats too."

I grinned and shook my head. "Leave it to Ricardo to think of those bloody cats as he's dying," I said, trying to stifle a chuckle.

Macuya smiled for the first time. "They were like children to him."

"Aye, they were," I agreed. "We'll look after them, and we'll look after you, mate." We stayed by Ricardo's side for a while in silence. Finally, I asked him, "Have you ever seen anything like that, Macuya?"

"Seen anything like what?" he asked.

"The kraken."

The young sailor turned his head and looked off into the vast ocean as if he were deep in thought. "I have seen things like it," he replied. "Beasts that will make you awaken from your dreams screaming and wet with sweat."

I did not ask him to elaborate. Quite frankly, I didn't think I wanted to know. I left Macuya with his fallen captain, and then gathered up the surviving members of my crew. I climbed what was left of the quarter deck stairs and gazed upon the small group of men that were nearly all the family I had left.

"Gentlemen, please know that the death of your shipmates was not in vain," I said. "There are no words I can say now to express my gratitude to each and every one of you. Captain Trimble is dead and when the word spreads about what we—what *you* all did today... Well, there's not a pirate alive that will challenge us now, mates! We'll return to New Providence, we'll make repairs, and then we'll return to the sea, where all of us belong."

The men erupted in joyous applause. The sea was exactly where they would always belong.

The End

www.ingramcontent.com/pod-product-compliance
Lightning Source LLC
Chambersburg PA
CBHW032008170626
46807CB00006B/2708